CAMP NOTECH

JAMES ARTHUR

DP 31 Media

Camp NoTech
Copyright © 2025 by James Arthur

First Edition: September 2025

ISBN 979-8-9998602-0-0 (ebook)
ISBN 979-8-9998602-1-7 (paperback)

Published by DP 31 Media

To My Father,

The one who always pushed me to be creative at a young age, but also showed me too many horror movies at a young age.

CHAPTER ONE

"PHONES! PHONES! PHONES! PHONES! PHONES!"

I shut my eyes and shake my head. It is the same thing every time the campers are set to leave. You would think after five days, these kids would have weaned themselves off the addiction. Not the case. As soon as I step on the bus with The Box, they go crazy. It is like they learned nothing this past week. Nope. As soon as they get a hint of the phones, they are like moody, pale-faced vampires looking for blood; wonderful texting blood. After working at Camp NoTech for the past ten weeks, I fully understand why parents send their children here.

The drug is technology.

This last day's craze is nothing compared to the first day they arrive. You would think someone had died. Watching them hand over their phones during the opening ceremony has become the highlight of the week for me and the other counselors. For some of them, I really wonder, even though the camp is called Camp NoTech, and they have been told from the beginning, "no phones," if some part of them still think we are joking.

It is no joke.

Miss Loretta does not joke about technology.

It is forbidden.

All 100 campers, if we have a full week, line up on a gravel pathway and make their way down to the amphitheater. The amphitheater has ten rows divided into two sections, where each cabin takes one row. My ten boys from the dramatic arts take their spot on the front right. We have to sit in the front because Adam and BB, with their sports cabin, get to sit in the back. Somewhere in the world, someone must have decided that all the athletes and cool guys need to sit in the back. I wonder what the average GPA would be if all athletes and cool guys sat in the front. A scientific study should be done.

One at a time, each camper walks to the front and places their Precious in The Box. It's sort of like you are at your own funeral and have to face your own body staring back at you. A sort of death happens in them, death to technology. No one truly understands how much they rely on these little devices until they are removed from their lives. Here is the catch: it really wouldn't make a difference if they kept them all week or not.

There is ZERO reception at Camp NoTech.

There is ZERO technology at Camp NoTech.

No cell reception. No Wi-Fi. No wired internet. Not even dial-up. There is NOTHING. The only line to the outside world is the landline phone locked in Ms. Loretta's office. No one has a key except Ms. Loretta. She will never let the key out of her sight.

Miss Loretta does not like technology.

It goes even further. No televisions. No computers. No Screens. No... Well, you get it.

No Tech.

I have seen everything this summer: campers crying, campers angry, campers trying to put fake phones in the box. One girl even went on a hunger strike on the first day of camp, hoping it would get her phone back. It did not work. The ceremony is supposed to represent them giving up their technology for the week. I didn't think it would exactly be like Abraham trying to sacrifice Isaac. There is a reason we called the phones "Their Precious." Gollum-like insanity follows for the first few hours. For some, it is days before their hands stop twitching. You can even watch campers keep reaching for phantom phones all the time. The nervous reaction to reach for something, to find that it is not there.

"NORM!"

My name snaps me back to reality. Tommy Hitts is standing on his seat, yelling at me. Stupid Tommy Hitts. He must really have an issue with technology. Either that or his parents didn't want him around for reasons known and unknown. He has been our camper for three weeks now. Part of the Adam Bombs, the sports cabin. Hitts is everything Adam loves in his cabin: 6'4" as a sophomore in high school, sharp as a whip, brown buzzed hair, and built "country strong," like Adam loves to say. After three weeks here, Hitts thinks he is a counselor himself.

"NORM!" Hitts yells again. "Phones!"

"Chill out, Hitts. You know the drill."

I take The Box, shiny and gold, and start to pass out the phones. Before I do, I tease them a little, acting like the phones are gone. Most of the campers know I am joking, but for others, it's another chance to see them sweat. Gold for the dramatic arts. My color all summer. The grubby hands of the campers are twitching as they wait for the first hit of a screen. One particular red-headed girl is near tears at the joy of being reunited. I give hers to her first, and she screams with joy.

Here is my favorite part. I wait and look as she powers it up.

"What the...? Where are my texts?" Here comes the waterworks. I can only imagine how much she has waited all week for this moment. She starts moving the phone around the bus, desperate for the connection. Now she stands on the seat and leans out the window, trying to get service. I catch her and bring her back in before she collapses entirely out the window. She fights me, crawling back toward the window. She is fiening hard.

"Stretch out there all you want." Hitts laughs. "You won't get any reception until we are out of the valley. At least ten miles." You can tell Hitts knows the routine. He powers his on like everyone else, but then plops it on the seat.

"Ten miles!" The red-headed girl screams. I would not have been surprised to hear her cry out, "MY PRECIOUS." I am on the verge of laughter as I watch the barrage of emotions on her face. Sadness, anger, more anger, back to sadness, then finally depression. It is going to be a long ten miles for her. I am sure she will stare at the screen the whole ten miles.

I shake my head again, and I continue the phone pass out. I hate this job. It's supposed to rotate among all of us counselors, but shockingly, every time it's Adams' turn, he "is busy with a sports emergency." So, I have been stuck most of the weeks getting the duty of returning the Precious to the campers.

"Thanks for everything this summer, Norm."

Raven Giles. For all the crap I had to put up with this summer, the Raven Gileses of the world are the reason this has been worth it. Skinny, black hair shaved to one side, eight piercings in her face alone, she was the star of the last two weeks. Sings like an angel and can act like an Oscar winner already. Being a senior in high school, I have gotten closer to her than most of the other campers. She is already better than I am, but she is gracious enough to take my teachings.

"Raven, you are amazing. Beyond talented." She gives me one of her rare smiles. We exchange quick hugs again. I already have her number and promised to text as soon as camp is finished for me. She will not be a camper for long. She will be a friend. I leave her and move on. She hasn't even glanced at her phone. She just tosses it in her bag. She is a rare bird. I have already recommended her to Miss Loretta as a future counselor.

All phones are passed out, and I take one last glance at the final group of campers. Only Raven and Hitts acknowledge me, as everyone is frantically finding something to do on their phones. No texts and no calls does not mean no games. Or pics. Or videos. I don't think they care what they are doing as long as it is on a phone.

I hop off and watch as the bus takes off down the road. The dust flies up as it slowly moves its large yellow frame at fifteen miles an hour. The road leading out of the valley away from Camp NoTech is long and steep. It must be driven slowly. Too many times this summer, I have been forced to take the road at breakneck speed. Adam only knows one speed. Not fast, but "uber fast," as he calls it. I watch the dust fade away and watch the bus until I can't see it anymore. I think about the first day I came down the Orioro (one road in, one road out).

I pulled in front of the main house in my old blue, beat-up '72 Chevy pickup. The pride and joy my father left to me a few years before. My dad had passed down many different things to me, but the truck has to be the best. I love it and treat it like the priceless work of art it is. One of the best things I love about working at Camp NoTech this summer is not having to drive it all summer. I worked all my free time at a nasty fast food restaurant so I could afford to keep her in pristine condition. It was immaculate. Nothing I loved more in the world than this truck. Well, maybe my mom, but the truck is a close second. So close, there is actual jealousy from my mom.

The truck holds memories of my father and me. Early memories of apple picking, filling the entire truck bed with apples. Drive-in movies from as early as I can remember. We would pop our own popcorn, put it in brown grocery bags, and then sit in the back of the truck. The truck is more than transportation.

I make my way into the main house, pausing at the top of the stairs to take in my surroundings. Not much different than when I came to the interview six months ago. The main house sits in the middle of the camp. The surrounding areas hold our cabins, dining hall, activities building, and storage shed. I couldn't see it from where I was, but I knew the lake was down the hill to the west. The only two other buildings are where the staff members live who help Miss Loretta all summer.

My flashback memory continues as I think about entering the house for the first time. The main level of the house was empty when I walked in. I am an hour early, and I guess Miss Loretta is elsewhere preparing for our orientation. Everything is just as I remembered. Walls covered with pictures of camp groups representing each week at Camp NoTech. Four years now, ten weeks each year, forty pictures. Couches and love seats take up most of the room, with a giant armor off to the side that I know holds every possible game you could imagine.

"This is your weekend hangout," Miss Loretta explained to me. "I bought the nicest furniture money could buy. Since you guys will only go off campgrounds once a week, it's important for you to have the best place to relax. The fridge here will always be packed with drinks, and the cabinets filled with snacks. Only the best for my family of counselors."

Having the best is something Miss Loretta believes in.

I start to make my way to an overstuffed chair when I hear music coming closer. The bumps of the bass are already shaking the windows as I glance out. All I see is dust coming toward me. I put my hand against the window and feel the vibrations. Whoever this is loves their music. And speed.

A few seconds later, a black convertible comes into view, going at a speed not recommended by our counselor handbook (uber fast). I do not even get a full view of the car until it comes to a stop next to my truck. The dust clears away, and I see a tall, blonde-haired guy get out of the convertible. He slings a bag over his shoulder and beeps the car lock, which is crazy since the top of the convertible is still down. He has only what I can describe as perfect wavy hair. He takes the sunglasses off his face and pushes them onto his head. He strides toward me. Dressed in a red shirt with red shorts and red sneakers, he moves with a confidence I could only dream of.

I move away from the window and try to act like I was doing something other than creeping on this guy. I rush back to the chair and sit, trying to look natural.

Perfect Blond Guy enters and stops right inside. He scans around the room much like I did. He finally notices me, and a big smile breaks out on his face.

"Bro!" He makes his way over to me, dropping his bag and lifting his hands in the air.

"Camp NoTech in the house."

I stand up and try to look as cool as I can. Too bad I am not cool. Perfect Blond Guy grabs me and embraces me into one of those awkward half-backpat-half-hugs.

"Bro, you're enormous!"

There it was. This single statement would go on to plague me all summer.

"You play ball, bro? O line? D line?" Huh? Guarding us QBs?" He starts playfully punching me in the stomach.

"No. I am the theater guy."

"Theatre? Nah, bro, you need to get on the field, Norm."

I stand there. The same question I have gotten all my life. Being big means you must play football. There is no way you could possibly not play it. No way you would rather be on stage. No way you get the same thrill and rush athletes get on the field. Therefore, I hate football.

"Wait, what? Norm?"

"Yeah, bro! Ya know, NORM! Enormous? Norm? Everybody knows your name?"

"But my name is not Norm, it's—"

"NORM! I love it."

He pulls me into another hug-pat as if this is the greatest thing in the world.

"I'm Adam, man."

Adam Jacobs. Twenty-two. Perfect blonde hair. Perfect white teeth. Frat boy at Mountain College. Lifeguard and sports. Leader of Cabin 1, the Adam Bombs. My new "bro."

You probably guessed by now, but my name is not Norm.

CHAPTER TWO

The bus is finally out of view, and the summer is done. No more campers. In less than 24 hours, I will head home, spend two weeks, and then return to school for my sophomore year. After being away for ten weeks, I am sure my mom is going to make me stay home and spend the entire time with her. She has done well since my dad died, keeping herself busy. My father left us with plenty of money, but Mom has started working part-time to have something to do. Plus, there is always church, volunteering, and gossip.

I head into the main house to escape the heat. Miss Loretta likes nice things, and that includes air-conditioning, which is awesome. All cabins and buildings are ice cold, and I love it. If I had to rank things again, it would be Mom, truck, and air-conditioning. There are very few things better in life than AC. I fall into the chair and close my eyes. I am exhausted. Ten weeks in a row of camp is beyond tiring. Once cleanup day is done, I may spend the next two weeks sleeping. I am looking forward to not having a schedule. There is always somewhere to be and something to do when you are at camp. Still, a little sadness hits me. It was a great summer. I am sure my fellow counselors would agree with me.

I hear Andrei before I see Andrei. This is always the case with Andrei.

"Glory be the day! I don't have to wear this hideous gray shirt anymore this summer! Andrei does not do gray." Andrei makes his way into the house with Lin tagging along as she always does.

"Andrei, it is not like anyone has been uploading pics of you all summer. No one is going to know about your gray summer."

"I will know, Lin Ai. I will know. Andrei has a standard to live up to no matter where he is, and this..." Andrei rips off his shirt and throws it across the room, "This gray shirt does not live up to Andrei's standard." I keep my eyes closed, but I laugh because this same ritual has played out each Friday this summer.

"Andrei needs to be free." I don't even need to open my eyes because I know. Andrei has just completed his clothing ritual by stripping off the grey shorts as well. Andrei has no trouble being free in front of others. There is less body fat on him than on anyone else at camp. He proudly shows off his lean, shark white body to everyone who will see. This week, the hair is orange. Last week it was green. Next week it will be something different. Andrei is something different.

Dark-haired Lin Ai has been an odd pairing to Andrei all summer, but we have all come to realize the calming effect she brings to him. She seems to get Andrei in a way no one else has. She is like the Andrei whisperer. While Andrei catapults his underwear-wearing self onto the plush couch, Lin lays her books all over the table, though she has no more science and math campers to teach. I don't know what she will be working on now, but she is always working on something. She had her campers spend their entire summer working with her. They would all gather around a table in the dining hall and work. I could never figure out what the work was, but they worked away. All Science. All Math. All day.

"Andrei's ready to party tonight!" he yells and lets a WHOO! fly out. This, too, is no surprise. Andrei is always ready to party. Everything is a party to him. Each morning, it is a breakfast party, followed by a lunch party, a beach party at the lake, and finally a dinner party. Andrei makes everything into a party." I don't answer, so I know what is coming next.

"Hello! Earth to Norm. Don't make Andrei show you some love." Andrei likes to show love to everyone. It really is an excuse for him to jump on you while he is naked.

"WHOO. Party," I say in a very tired manner.

"Now, Norm. Look at Andrei."

I open my eyes and close them again. Andrei is now positioned with his legs spread wide on the table across from me.

"Take Andrei in Norm. In all his glory!"

Andrei is proud.

"I guess I am ready to party," I say with my eyes still closed. Tight. "Though I think I would rather just sleep tonight. Tomorrow is going to be long."

"I concur," Lin adds. "I am not looking forward to cleaning all the cabins and campgrounds. I need to get back to my studies. I have three weeks to get ready for school."

"Don't worry about tomorrow, dear. Andrei will make it fun." I wait for it. I hear Andrei stand on the table and... "It will be a cleaning party!"

I chuckle hard and try to catch some rest before everyone else joins us. Looks like I am going to need my energy for tonight. Last night's party is legendary. Adam has talked all summer about it. Adam and BB are the only two returning staff from the previous year. BB seems indifferent to most things, but Adam raves about the party like it is the single greatest thing ever. Actually, when Adam is excited, then everything is the single greatest thing ever.

As if on cue, I hear two large elephant feet making their way up the stairs. Standing 6'8" and weighing close to 320 pounds, Billy Bonner, aka BB, is a superhuman specimen. I still wonder what an all-American football star from Arkansas Tech is doing here. He could be spending his summer anywhere he wished, but he chose Camp NoTech. He seems to love it. Miss Loretta loves him. He brings some added publicity to Camp NoTech. I always think BB likes not being accessible to the media, agents, and coaches.

He opens the door, and his massive frame enters the room. Unlike Andrei, he keeps his too-tight blue shirt and shorts on. Like always, he is wearing his blue whistle. The blue looks nice on his Samoan skin. Miss Loretta does not like tattoos, but if you're an all-American star working at your camp, then you don't mind the arm sleeve BB sports. All the ladies during the summer were in love with BB, but when he shows no interest in them, Adam is ready to enjoy all the attention. Bob plops himself down in the chair next to me. I don't try to engage him because BB rarely talks. Unless he is yelling at campers during his practices, BB is not social.

I continue to rest as much as I can while the others waste time. It has been a learning experience on how to entertain yourself without a phone. It has not bothered me much since I feel like I am creative enough. But others went through heavy withdrawals in the first week. Andrei barely made it to the first time off camp campgrounds before losing his mind. He spent the whole first week hounding Adam on how to get the key from Miss Loretta!

Andrei and Lin have been joined by another camp duo: Belle and Davis. A summer fling is one thing, but these two have been all over each other this summer. Davis is the rugged Hispanic outdoorsman who leads the hiking, rock climbing, and camping track this summer. While Davis is chill and laid back, he is nothing compared to Belle Peterson. Belle's long flowing blonde hair and porcelain white skin match perfectly with the term "hippy chick." Nothing ever bothers Belle. Her art classes this summer are notorious for starting late and running to whenever Belle feels "the cosmos has told us we are done." Cook hates this. She runs a tight ship in the dining hall and is always having to leave food out for Belle's group. Cook is old, cranky, and large. I wouldn't mess with her. Yes, everyone calls her Cook. She has a name, but Cook is who she is here. Like me.

I am Norm.

DeMarcus is in the main house kitchen preparing the food for tonight. I don't even worry about what it is because everything he makes is awesome. He is going to be the next Bobby Flay. At least that is what he tells everyone. Demarcus Sims can make canned soup, canned chicken, and canned beans into a quality dish. He has opened my world this summer to things I never thought I would like. Not only him but the campers he has taught, too. Sharing a cabin with some of his campers has been amazing. It means all the left-overs come to me...I mean...to us. I can make toast, and that is about it.

Can you burn water?

Then there is Bliss. Again, I don't even have to open my eyes to know when Bliss is curled up in the bay window, writing or reading. Bliss is always writing and reading. I'm the closest to her here at Camp NoTech. The passion with which she taught her campers this summer equals my passion for the arts.

Bliss and I spent many nights talking and dreaming big dreams.

"Wouldn't it be great if we can move to New York after we graduate, Norm? Move there and live in a small loft while

I write and you make it on Broadway. I can already see it, Norm. We can do this."

Bliss is the happiest person I have ever met. I know for a fact I would never have made it through this summer without her. Lying under the stars at night, I really could believe we could make it in New York.

Bliss is the perfect friend. She is small but strong. With long, dark brown hair and beautiful skin, she is going to make someone happy someday. But not me. Bliss doesn't like guys, and that is fine with me. For once, I can have a relationship with a girl and not stress about feelings I can never seem to stop.

"Normy. We are going to do big things, you and I. We are a team."

"I believe you, Bliss."

That night was special. It ended with a kiss on the cheek. That kiss meant more to me than if I had kissed hundreds of girls before. Which I haven't. I haven't kissed any girls.

But I wish I could kiss Manda.

Manda Ray is perfect in every way. That is what has been running through my mind all summer. Perfect black hair, perfect tanned skin, perfect body, perfect eyes, perfect lips.

But, of course, perfect attracts perfect, and guys my size are not perfect.

Adam is perfect.

CHAPTER THREE

All summer it has been the summer of Adam. Who is the most popular counselor? Adam. Who is Cook's favorite? Adam. Who does Miss Loretta trust when she leaves camp? Adam. Who gets to spend all summer kissing Manda? Adam. Who gets to do more than kissing with Manda? Adam. Who declared themselves my best friend this summer? For some strange reason, Adam.

Now we sit here about to have our last hurrah for the summer, and all I can think about is how much less perfect I am than Adam. What doesn't help is that he thinks we are the best of friends. Nothing is more frustrating than not liking someone when they like you back. Even I am not sold 100% on his adoration for me. Bliss always tells me not to worry about it, and she thinks Adam is more genuine than I give him credit for. She claims my undying love and pining for Manda all summer has jaded my view. I tell her she is wrong, but she is rarely wrong.

"My dear, wonderful counselors. Oh, I have adored you all summer."

Miss Loretta is standing before us one last time. We are all sitting in the luxury furniture she has provided for us.

"Tonight is my chance to show you how much I appreciate you all. We have some wonderful food prepared for you by our own DeMarcus. DeMarcus, won't you take a bow?" DeMarcus stands up as we all applaud him. Not one for attention, he sits and gives the floor back to Miss Loretta.

"Now, my dears, as you know, electronics are frowned upon here at Camp NoTech, but tonight I have made an exception." Now that gets our attention. We sit up a little straighter, wondering where Miss Loretta is going with this. Maybe we will get out of camp for the party and use our phones or a game system. I could really shoot up enemies right now.

"When I went to town this morning, I rented you guys your own...karaoke system!"

Now I don't know if it is the fact that we are at the end of a crazy summer or if it's the lack of technology, but when she says karaoke system, you would have thought Miss Loretta said, "You all get a new car!" We went nuts. Well, all except BB, who really doesn't go nuts any time he is off the field.

"Andrei loves karaoke!' Thankfully, he is dressed now and not still in his underwear. He runs and jumps on BB's lap. Another ongoing Andrei tradition this summer: His love affair with BB. Andrei broke up with his boyfriend before camp and by the end of the week had already declared his love for the football star. To Andrei, it was a match made in heaven.

"Andrei is going to sing you a love song tonight, BB." BB just smiles and tosses Andrei to the next seat over on top of Lin. Tosses him like he was nothing. Andrei lets out a yelp.

"Boo! Andrei just needs some love." He plants a big kiss on Lin. Lin acts like it is the worst thing ever, but we all know

Lin enjoys it. Andrei is very free with his kisses. I have been on the receiving end of many this summer.

"Now, if one of you dears could please set up the karaoke machine, I will be on my way." Every Friday night, Miss Loretta disappears for all hours. She thinks she is being sly, but we all know she is getting it on somewhere with someone. She is secretive about what she does, and that is fine. She is with us all week and deserves to go out.

"Norm will set it up. My bro is smart like that." I am not surprised by this. Adam thinks I can fix or set up anything. This was established in our first week when the smoke alarm in Cabin 1 (Adam Bombs number !) was beeping like crazy, and Adam came running into Cabin 2 (2 Be or Not 2 Be) trying to find me to fix it. Of course, I don't know anything about fixing anything. But I was able to get the beeping to stop by taking out the battery. Since then, "Norm, my bro, is smart!" Ice Cream machine, the shower in Cabin 9, Manda's sandals. I was looked upon to fix it all.

Really, all I did was find Cohen.

Sure enough, I glance back, and there he is standing against the wall. He gives me a nod, and I know the karaoke machine will be set up. Cohen is the camp's everyman. He does all the fixing of things, he finds things, and he is even a nurse. Standing only 5'2", he is small but mighty. The boss of the camp. Even more than Miss Loretta. Even though he has graying hair and wears overalls 24/7, we all give him the utmost respect.

Miss Loretta makes her rounds, giving us all hugs before she takes off for the night. DeMarcus sets out the food. We all gather around the giant wooden table, and I have to admit it feels special. With Cohen at the head like our father, we settle in. I am between Adam on one side and Bliss on the other side. I know I am in for a night.

"Andrei is rocking some jams tonight." We all laugh as we dig into our first course. DeMarcus has prepared an amazing French onion soup. The first bite nearly makes me faint. Beyond delicious.

"At least we won't have to worry about Able Dunn tonight, bro," Adam says, shoveling in his soup. Adam Bombs do everything fast! "Your singing will drive away anything that comes near here."

Cohen gives a little chuckle.

"Why did you have to say his name? You know, Andrei gets scared." Andrei lays his head on BB's shoulder. "Will you save me from Able, BB?"

"Sure."

With that, BB has spoken.

"Tell us more about Able Dunn," Bliss says, looking at Cohen. We have all spent the summer hearing the tales of Able. The man who lost his land, the camp is built on.

"Well, what can I say that hasn't already been said?" Cohen slides his bowl back to make room for the ribeye and vegetable medley that is the second course. He takes his time getting the story started. He slices into his steak and takes a slow bite. He seems to be enjoying it like it's the last steak he will ever eat.

"Is it true that the Main House is built right on top of his family grave?"

"Well, Bliss. There is so much now that is legend, it is hard to determine what is fact." Again, Cohen takes a bite and chews it for a long time. I really can't blame him there. The steak is amazing. I hate vegetables, so I haven't touched them. "Bro! Eat your veggies! We got to get you in shape." I have heard that plenty this summer. But thankfully, Adam is not focused on me. He is shuffling steak into his mouth. Cut, stab, eat. Over and over.

"Here is the story, and I should know since I have been with Miss Loretta from the beginning." Cohen pushes his steak away, content with being the storyteller of this dinner party. I push my plate away after my steak is done. Adam reaches right over and takes my veggies off my plate. We are best bros, after all.

"The Dunn family had owned this land for many generations. Able's great-great-grandfather settled here and made a modest living. He had some animals and some crops, but his main trade was survival training." A dessert is placed in front of me this time. Key lime pie. Cohen ignores his and continues.

"The Dunns were known for taking this survival training to the extreme. Pushing the limits on surviving. Taking participants out for longer and longer times. For many years, they were successful. People would travel from all over the country to learn how to push their own limits."

At this point, we have all stopped eating, fully entranced by the tale. Even Andrei is calm.

"Then, when Able's father, Mackie Dunn, took over the land and the business, he had these crazy ideas that the government was unstable. He would preach to his customers that a collapse was coming soon."

"This paranoia and obsession grew. You have to remember this was at the height of the Cold War. People everywhere were afraid that the big bomb would drop at any moment. But Mackie Dunn took it too far. He would take people down into this valley to prepare them anyway he felt fit."

I dropped my fork. Pie had lost my interest.

"He had this thing about gas masks. Wore them everywhere. He made his wife, Able's mom, and Able himself wear them everywhere. They were never allowed to take them off. Able was ridiculed everywhere. No one was allowed to set foot on the Dunn property without a gas mask. When they were on a survival trek, if they took them off, they were dead. Mackie made them stay right where they were when they took the mask off."

"A senator came with his family one weekend. This guy, the senator, was trying to cash in on the paranoia going on. He figured if he could get some good shots of him and his family preparing for the end, people would flock to him. It was him, his wife, his teenage son, and two twin girls, both aged 8."

I checked around the rest of the table, and everyone was still. Even Adam, who never takes anything seriously, had stopped eating my pie. I hadn't even seen him take it from me. Cohen had our full attention.

"Mackie took the senator out on the trek. Able, all of 13, went with them. It was too cold for people to be out there for long periods of time. It was well below freezing during the day, and even colder at night. Mackie would keep people out for hours at a time. Making them gather and build fires, capture game, and survive. The tale says that three days into the trek, one of the twins lost it. She was in a full panic and pulled off her mask. The other twin panicked, seeing this, and took off their mask as well."

"Mackie declared the girls dead. That is how it went. The senator and Mackie fought. Things came to blows, and the senator gathered his family and took off back to the Dunn's land. They never made it. Their bodies were never found. Mackie was finished."

"The news had a field day. Declared him insane, and all his extreme ways came to light. A hearing was called, and Mackie was declared guilty. As hard as Able and his mother tried, they couldn't keep the business going. They slowly started selling land back to the bank to keep going. This lasted for years. Able's mom passed away soon after his 30th birthday.

He buried her with his father right here. Yes, where this house was built.

Then, Able disappeared.

"Not for long but for months at a time. He would be gone, then come back, sell some more of the land, and then disappear again. Rumor has it he was finishing the shelter his father had started. At least it was believed to be the shelter because get this: Able never stopped wearing the gas mask. Never. All those years. No one has seen his face since he was a small boy."

"What happened to Mackie?" I ask softly. "How'd he die?"

"In jail. Shortly after he was convicted, he was found hanging, wearing a gas mask."

"Poor Able." I looked and saw Bliss with tears in her eyes. Cohen nodded.

"Poor Able is right. Finally, he sold off all the land to the bank. That was it. He was gone. Ten years ago, Miss Loretta bought a large chunk of it and built this camp. No one has seen Able since that last time at the bank."

"Except when he is out here terrorizing the camp, right?" I see Manda slap Adam.

"What? I'm serious. You mean none of you have ever thought about it? The times the buildings are vandalized? The animals all ending up dead? Am I the only one who doesn't see this?"

"Adam." Cohen pauses. "There is no Able out there. The vandalism is always by the campers. The animals were a virus. That is all. Every year, someone tries to claim that they see Able late at night on the campgrounds. But it is not true. It is false."

"Sure, bro. Let's all keep telling each other that. Until one night, Able Dunn comes and guts us all." I shake my head. Adam's stupidity still amazes me.

"Stop saying that. You're scaring Andrei."

"I've been all over this valley," Davis chimes in. "I am out there all summer. All the trails, all the hills, camped there all night. I never saw anything. Nada. There is no hidden shelter, no killer on the loose, nothing of Able Dunn."

"Which would be what he would want, bro. Think about it." Adam's face takes on an off-key look. Maybe it is the shadows around or the fact that Cohen just told us this freaky story, but Adam has our attention. He leans forward, his hands gripping the table. I see the muscles flexing.

"If you wanted to be left alone and wanted no one to know where you are, then a shelter in the woods is perfect, especially if it is underground. He comes out when he needs something. He steals from us. He tries to scare us. He wants us gone. I mean, the Main House is built on the grave of his parents. He lives underground, in a bunker. The bunker is probably set up to survive the end of the world. No telling how long he can last there."

He stops talking. We are all just sitting silently. I ponder what Adam is saying. Could Able Dunn still be out there? Could he be the one who is always behind the unexplained things that happen each summer at Camp NoTech? Out there still carrying on the lessons his father instilled in him? I look at everyone who is still looking at Adam.

"Just imagine, bros. Able is still out there. Ready...to kill us...ALL!" Adam is shaking the table and screaming, with plates and food going everywhere. He stops screaming and is now laughing like crazy.

"You jerk! Don't do that to Andrei!"

"Come on!" I yell at Adam. "Able Dunn is about the dumbest thing I have ever heard of." The table is still rattling, and I am trying to calm myself down. We all start throwing things at Adam. Food, napkins, silverware, he is so happy with himself, scaring us like that. Even Manda looks annoyed with him.

"There is no way some guy has been living out in a shelter for 20 years. You bros are just wussies." Adam is still laughing to himself, and soon we are all joining in with him. It does seem silly. Adam rises out of his seat and holds up his glass.

"Now, let's get this party started!"

CHAPTER FOUR

Time: 8:46 P.M.
Location: Cook's Private Quarters

Cook is already four beers deep into her nightly routine. Seated in her chair, she is slowly dozing off, watching reruns of "Golden Girls." She laughs to herself again, thinking about how jealous these campers would have been all summer, knowing she has a TV.

She questions again why she spends her summers working at this stupid camp. Well into her 50s with constant back pain and arthritis, she stays retired year-round. She doesn't need to work, doesn't need the money. Boredom is really the reason. You can only sit around your lake house for so long before you start to go a little crazy.

She lights another smoke and pops open her fifth beer. She takes a long swig and sighs. Another summer is done. Tomorrow will be time to pack up and head home. She looks around, thinking about all the work that needs to be done to get ready to go. She laughs again, as she knows she can get one of the counselors to do it for her.

Her private quarters are top-notch for a 10-week summer gig. But, then again, Miss Loretta is paying her an outrageous amount of money. Seven years into the gig, and she still can't believe her luck, especially when there is always some young chef eager to help her. One of the perks.

She reclines back in her chair and starts to relax some more. Even though there is a nice king-size bed, she loves her burgundy recliner. It is called King Size, and her 5'10 400-pound frame fits in it like a warm hug. Besides the bed, the chair, and the TV, she also enjoys her own private kitchen and bathroom. Thoroughly trashed from the summer, but she doesn't care. This isn't her home. Besides, there is something nice about just throwing things anywhere she pleases.

The kids are little twits anyway. The problem with Miss Loretta charging so much for the camp is that we get these entitled brats who demand every little thing. "Where is my double soy half mocha infused with lemon grass latte?" How she could have strangled those little skanks. Take away their phones, and caffeine is their only addiction left.

But that is done. Finally, the lake house is calling her back home.

But Cook was being watched.

Nothing sexual about it. More like a hunger to look into someone's world. The tall figure is standing and peering into the only window that adorns the tiny quarters. It is lucky Cook is facing toward the TV and doesn't notice the breath fogging her window.

Soon, she is snoring.

The way the little cabin is set up, the door is behind her. No reason to lock it. Why would she? Anyone who would come into the place would instantly want to leave when they entered. Weeks of leftover food and dirty laundry have created a smell that could only be described as putrid. Cook only bathes once a week. Too much work. By the end of the day, her feet hurt her too bad.

But when you are wearing a gas mask, no smell bothers you.

Stepping in slowly, he feels the crunch under his feet of takeout containers and rotten food. He moves closer into the room. The narrow spaces that the mask allows him to see through don't show much. He turns his head around, taking in the scene. Humans are filth. Why should we be worried about the end of the world when humans are going to kill the planet?

Cook snorts and adjusts in her chair. He stands by her chair, taking in the scene on the television. The glow of the set makes him seem even larger than he is. Moving his head downwards, he observes the lady in the chair. With a glass bottle in one hand and a burning cigarette in the other, she is oblivious to his presence.

He shuffles over through the trash to the small kitchen. All the counters are covered in filth. Bugs are flying and crawling around, so he moves the trash with his hand. He knocks some of it on the floor, uncovering a large knife. Gripping the handle tightly, he lifts it and looks at it closely. He can see the reflection of the gas mask coming off the blade.

He raises it high and stabs it into the counter.

The noise wakes Cook. She looks around in a daze, trying to figure out where the noise came from. She sits up in the chair, puts out her cigarette, and pushes her feet down. She looks around and starts breathing. Standing there looking at her is a man. She freezes, and the only thing that she can think about is how big he is. At least 6'10", he seems to be muscular, but she really can't tell since he is wearing a red and black checkered jacket with black pants. He has long, dirty black hair hanging down past his shoulders. The ends are choppy and crooked, like it has seen many years of being cut.

He is wearing a gas mask. Dark green. She has not seen one of these since she was a girl, back when all kids were required to learn how to wear and use one. His breathing is barely audible through it. He steps toward her with his black boots again, crunching the containers on the floor.

Cook stands up. Her knees almost give out. She is not used to having to rise so fast. He starts to stalk toward her. She glances down and notices the knife in his hand. It is a good knife. Miss Loretta only buys her the best. A flash of light gleams off the blade. Cook looks at the TV and sees a commercial for a knife that can cut through anything.

While he is moving slowly, Cook is trying to move as fast her body will take her. She moves backwards until she hits the wall. She feels the picture frame poking her back. The same art she has stared at for the past seven years, a picture of a girl running with a kite through a field. She wishes now she were fast enough to run away. But the years of smoking, drinking, and eating what she wants has left her barely mobile.

"Who are you?" she stammers as he makes his way closer to her. "What do you want? Why are you here?" He is close enough now that she can feel the heat coming off his body.

He stops close enough that he is sort of resting on her stomach. The mask is right in front of her face, and it strikes her as odd that she could kiss it right now if she wanted to. The tears start to fall. Snot is coming out of her nose as fear is taking control.

"Please. Please. What do you want?" She is speaking softly and trying to get a glimpse of his eyes through the mask. It is useless. This is where she will die.

He takes the knife and plunges it into her stomach. He drives it in deep, far into her large stomach, to where the blade is completely hidden. She lets out a soft cry. He pulls it out and back in again. Cook can hear a small brunt escaping from the mask with each thrust.

Slow each time. His mask is pressed against her face, and his whole body moves onto her with each plunge.

Blood is gushing out on the floor, all over his gloved hands. Over and over, he drives it into her. Harder and faster has the plunges move in a rhythm, taking her life from her. With one final push, he drives the knife so deep into her that his hand is in her stomach. He leaves it there, letting the knife come to a resting place as he watches her eyes go blank.

He takes the blade out and drops it on the floor. He steps back, boots covered in blood. Cook's body falls to the ground to join the rest of the trash sitting there. He backs away and exits the cabin. The last thing he sees is the glow of the TV coming off her face.

CHAPTER FIVE

I don't drink alcohol. Therefore, whenever everyone around me is drinking, I just marvel at how stupid they are. Take right now, for instance. I am back sitting in my comfy chair. All around is craziness. As soon as Cohen departed, Adam and Andrei left and returned with several large boxes of adult beverages. They have been saving all the stuff they caught the campers with all summer. Since the campers are wealthy, there is some high-end liquid that the boys have been eying for weeks.

Currently, Andrei is entertaining us with his fifth pop song in a row. He has hit the sauce hard, so all his words are slurred, his moves not in sync with the beat. Davis and Belle are doing what Davis and Belle do best: being all over each other. Right now, she has Davis straddled, her tongue down his throat. At least they are clothed this time. Lin is laughing and cheering on Andrei. Adam has Manda on the makeshift dance floor dancing up against her. I shake my head as I watch this, pushing the envy down, like I have all summer.

DeMarcus is passed out on the couch, and BB hasn't moved since dinner, sitting off by himself, drinking beer after beer. There's no way to tell if he is drunk or not. He shows no emotion.

The only saving grace to me is Bliss. Sitting next to me, she has been sporting the same glass of wine the entire time. Like always, she is writing or drawing in her journal. I never know how to act at parties like this. They always start fine, but as more alcohol is consumed, the more conversations turn stupid. My eyes wander back to Manda and Adam. A little fury rises in the chest. I wish Manda knew that she could do better.

Better like me.

I was the first to welcome Manda to Camp NoTech. Adam and BB had just taken off from the Main House to claim their cabins from the previous summer, and I was waiting for Miss Loretta to show up. Something that we ended up waiting for quite a bit this summer. Miss Loretta likes nice things, but a watch is not one of them. One time, we were waiting forever, like hours, late into the night. We were all getting more and more frustrated as the night went on, finally she came in just to make sure we know which campers are ours tomorrow. Everyone was beyond livid.

I was standing on the porch when I saw a white SUV making its way down the Orioro. It barely seems to stop when a blonde girl hops out. Her feet are barely on the ground when the SUV spins around and heads back out. The blonde stands there for a bit, watching the vehicle leave. Even from here, I can see that she has been crying.

She picks up her suitcase and looks up at the house. I am standing right there, but I can't tell if she even notices me. Her shoulders shrug, and she starts toward me. Stopping at the bottom of the steps, she finally seems to notice that I am there.

"Welcome to Camp NoTech," I say.

"Hey."

"Do you need some help with your suitcase?"

"Huh? Oh my bag! No, I can get it."

She makes her way up the rest of the stairs. With each step, I feel the sick feeling in my stomach grow. She is beautiful. Even with no makeup and puffy red eyes from crying, she is the prettiest girl I have seen.

I instantly clam up.

"So, do I go inside?" I know she is talking to me, but for some reason, the words that come to my mind don't come out of my mouth. Instead, I sort of nod and move my arm toward the door. Kind of like I am welcoming her to a show.

Smooth.

"I will take that as a yes." I follow her inside and bump into her as she has stopped.

"Uhwelluhiamsorry." The words come out fast. She turns and just smiles at me.

"It's OK. Sometimes I get lost in my head and don't notice others around me." While she is talking, I take in her face. She has light freckles on her face and a tiny scar on her upper lip. I try to fight the urge to look down, but I can't help it since she is wearing a low-cut shirt with no sleeves and cut off at her belly. The nausea grows.

"I'm Manda," she says, holding her hand out to me. I take it and shake it the best I can.

"Hi, I'm Manda."

"You're Manda, too?" She laughs at me. I am about to correct her when I hear noise coming from the back of the house.

"WHOA! Bro, what do we have here?" Adam and BB have returned. With that, Manda turns around, and that is that. It has been Adam ever since.

Turns out Manda is the lifeguard as well as a swim instructor. So, all summer, we are on two different tracks. While I spend all day inside working on the weekly performance, she is outside with Adam. It took about 5.5 seconds for them to latch onto each other.

"Thinking about Manda again?" I snap back to the present. Bliss has taken a break from her journal to notice me staring. "The summer is over. Let her go. Soon, you will be back in school. Adam will move on. Manda will move on. You should move on, too."

"I know. I wish I had any chance this summer to really get to talk to her. Every time I am around her, Adam is there, too." Just like now. Andrei is singing about getting real close, and they are practically inseparable.

"I don't think talking is all you wanted to do with her this summer." I play shocked and smack Bliss on the shoulder.

"Shut up. You want her just as much as me."

"Not my type at all." She is laughing now. I am so glad she is here to distract me from my Manda pains. Bliss has been there for me since Day 1.

We had all finally arrived and were sitting in the Main House. Adam already has Manda seated by him. He is telling her all about the camp and the fun they are going to have this summer. All the others are spread out. It is that awkward time before you really know anyone. We just sit there looking and making small talk. Not BB. BB doesn't do small talk.

I make a count in my head and come up with nine counselors. One is still missing. The man that I would know as Cohen is sitting in the back, leaning back in a chair. A large lady who Adam yelled "Cook" at when she walked in, is sitting on a chair by the window, smoking a cigarette.

We all stop talking when we hear a car pull up and stop in front of the house.

"I bet that is Miss Loretta." Adam hops up and heads to the front door, swinging it open.

"Miss Loretta, there you are!" He moves aside, and in walks Miss Loretta. She is actually how I remember her from my interview. She is either in her late 30s or her early 50s. You really can't tell. She is dressed in clothes too tight for her age, with a layer of makeup. She is not alone.

The girl who would become Bliss enters. While I don't have the same reaction as I did with Manda, she is beautiful. She looks around, taking in the scene. While others, like myself, would have been intimidated by walking into a room of strangers, she is relaxed, even confident. I instantly admire her.

"Oh, my dears, you are already here!" Miss Loretta looks thrilled like only she can. Adam engulfs her in a big hug, and BB stands to shake her hand. We all show Miss Loretta respect. At all times. All summer. While working at a camp is not unusual for college-age students, what Miss Loretta pays her counselors is unusual. As a first-time counselor, I am set to earn $1000 a week for 10 weeks. That is not including any gifts or tips that parents leave us for our work. As a third-year counselor, Adam is paid $2500 a week but took home over $10,000 more in tips last year. For this reason, we are always nice to Miss Loretta.

I see Bliss start to scan the room, looking for a seat. I regret choosing a love seat. At the same time, a love seat is great for two people. When you are someone my size, I take up a good 60% of the seat already.

"The only seat left is Norm over there, bro," Adam says, giving me a wink. I find myself turning red.

If Bliss notices, she doesn't let on. She walks straight over to me and sits down.

"Hey, Norm. We are going to be best friends this summer." She loops her arm into mine and smiles big at me.

Lin has now joined Andrei on the karaoke, belting out some old tunes about islands and their streams. They are making an odd drunk couple. Next to us, Davis and Belle are going at it. I see Belle start to lift her shirt.

"No, no, no, no." Bliss is up and pulling her away. "If you two want to have some fun, take it elsewhere." Belle is laughing while Bliss is trying to put her shirt back on. I try not to steal a glance at the pink bikini top she has on.

"Boo. You are no fun, Bliss," Belle pouts.

"Oh, I can be fun. But let's keep that fun behind closed doors."

"Come on, Davis. Take me to the lake. I feel like swimming."

"Your wish is my command." The two start stripping off their clothes and head out the door.

CHAPTER SIX

Time: 10:01 P.M.
Location: The Lake

Davis and Belle are already down to their swimsuits by the time they reach the lake. They stop once they get there to make out more. Davis turns, takes Belle by the hand, and leads her over to one of the lounge chairs.

He pushes her down and climbs on top. He starts to kiss her neck, moving his hands everywhere. Belle kisses him back. They are about to really get into it when they hear a SNAP. They both stop, sitting up and looking off into the woods.

"What was that?" Belle asks.

"I don't know." They sit there a while longer but hear nothing else. Davis moves back on top of Belle, and they continue where they left off.

SPLASH.

This time, Belle pushes Davis off and stands up, looking toward the lake.

"Did you hear that?"

"It's probably just a fish."

"A fish?" Belle has her two arms wrapped around her chest. She steps closer to the lake.

"Come on, babe. Come back here."

"Shhh. I'm trying to hear it again." Davis hops up and joins her. They both stop to listen. There are no more snaps, no more splashes. The only sound they hear is the gentle moving of the water.

"See, there is nothing out there."

"Maybe you're right. What I heard was larger than a fish, though."

"Don't worry about it. Come here." Davis grabs her back in his arms and kisses her gently on the cheek. He moves his hand down her backside when Belle pushes him away.

"I can't think about that right now," Davis groans and tries to pull her back in.

"I'm serious, Davis. The mood has passed."

"You're killing me." She starts to laugh at the puppy dog face he is giving her.

"We can still have fun. We don't always have to be naked to make it a blast."

Davis stands still, thinking over her comment.

"You're right. Let's go." He grabs her by the arm, and they run toward a ladder at the edge of the lake.

The ladder leads 20 feet to the very top. About halfway, there is a ledge that allows a person to climb out. At the top of it is a platform. It is used to jump off onto what is called the Blob. The Blob is a fixture at most camps. The giant inflatable sits on the lake surface. One person sits on the edge of the Blob, while the other jumps on, propelling the first person up in the air and into the lake. The blob itself is about 30 feet long and is the color of a rainbow.

They both get to the top and look out onto the lake.

"I disagree with you, by the way," Davis says.

"On what?"

"Everything is more fun naked." He reaches out and snatches the top of Belle. She covers herself and mocks shame. Davis takes off his shorts and tosses them down the ladder. Belle uncovers her chest and takes off her bikini bottoms.

"Who is going first?" she asks.

"You go down, and I will take the big leap. Then..." he says, pulling her close. "When we get in the water, we finish what we started."

"Deal."

Belle makes her way back down to the little ledge and stumbles out to the edge of the blob. She has to go slow, or you can fall right off. She settles on the edge.

"Go for it, Davis."

Davis runs off and jumps 10 feet down. He hits the blob in a cannonball, and Belle is shot off. She screams as she is flying through the air. She takes in the moon, the trees, and the man coming out of the lake.

As she descends, he comes out of the water. He pulls out a long spear and shoves it into her chest as she reaches the water. No sound escapes her, but she is coherent enough to stare into the eyes of the gas mask. The man drags the spear and Bliss down into the water. Blood has spilled, leaving a dark shape in the water.

Davis is screaming and celebrating the launch of Belle while trying to make his way to the front of the blob.

"That was awesome, babe. You went so high." He is looking down into the water, waiting for Belle to emerge. Nothing happens.

"Belle?' he hollers. "Belle! Where are you?" He is now

lying flat on his stomach. Holding on to one of the straps on the blob, he was leaning over as far as he could see. Scanning the water, he saw no sign of Belle. Letting go of the strap, he slips headfirst into the water.

He stays under for a bit. Being the outdoorsman that he was, he could hold his breath for a while. With only the moon to see, he realized it was useless. When he surfaced, he scanned around again. The only thing he can see is the light splashing off the surface of the lake. It takes a moment for his eyesight to adjust, and then he sees something.

About five yards away, he saw Belle's body on the surface of the water. She was face down.

"Belle! Belle! Are you OK?"

He swims over to her as fast as he can. He is able to touch the ground after a few feet and gain more momentum getting to her. When he reaches her, he turns her body over to see if she is OK.

She was dead. Her eyes froze in shock with a giant bloody hole through her torso.

"What? What is this?" Davis looks around, panicked, his arms and legs flailing as he turns and turns, looking. The moon moves behind the clouds, leaving only a little light. Thunder is heard off in the distance. A summer storm is coming.

Davis stops moving and looks again at Belle's body. He hears movement and looks, coming out of the water about three feet away, is a large figure. He is holding a spear.

Davis pushes Belle's body away and starts to run out of the water. Trying as he can to stay upright, he is slipping and falling as he reaches the edge. He turns and falls. The figure is standing above him. How did someone that big move that fast?

"No. No, no, no. Please." Davis tries to scramble back,

but the figure steps on his ankle, stopping him and crushing it at the same time. Davis screams in pain.

The man with the gas mask raises the spear and drives it into Davis' throat, silencing the scream. Davis' body is still twitching as the masked man drags the body, still attached to the spear, back into the water.

CHAPTER SEVEN

I sit there and watch as Adam tries to stay upright. Manda has to practically carry him over to the couch. He is mumbling something about being her best bro as she lays him down. She gets him halfway on the couch with his legs still dangling off.

I feel like I should get up to help her, but if she wants to be with him, then I think she should get used to this. It won't be their last drunken night together. It may not even be their first. She finally gets his whole body on the couch, and he is asleep before she even stands back up.

I see her survey the room. Lin and Andrei have finally ended their concert and are now drinking on the front porch. Demarcus left to put away the rest of the food. Bliss is curled up and asleep in the chair beside me. BB is still sitting off to the side, still drinking, still being quiet.

Manda makes her way over to me and sits on the ottoman in front of me. My legs are off to one side, but she still has plenty of room.

"He never can hold his liquor," she says, nodding over to the now drooling Adam. If I am not mistaken, I see a glimpse of annoyance in her eyes. I wouldn't blame her if she is. It can't be nice having your man drop dead drunk.

"I have never understood the appeal of being completely wasted," I tell her. I am still nervous speaking around her, but after a summer of being Adam's pal, it is easier. Even now, sitting here in front of me, the light of the lamp shining on her, she is beautiful.

"Yeah, it is not the greatest."

"Then why do people do it?" She tilts her head at me, acting like she has never even ponder this question before.

"I don't really know. For some, it is an escape. A way to forget their problems. For others, they need that extra push to be more themselves. For Adam, I think it starts as fun for him, and then he doesn't know when to stop." As if on cue, Adam gives a big snort and rolls over. "Being here this summer, maybe it's boredom?"

"The sad thing is he doesn't even need it," Manda says. "You know how crazy and fun he is normally. I tell him all the time he doesn't need to drink to be the life of the party."

I am taken aback by this statement. If you would have asked me, all Adam and Manda's relationship was a physical thing. I never thought they really talked. Like a real couple. Now it's my head that tilts as I ponder a question. One that kept me up at night during the summer. I haven't had more than four minutes alone with Manda to even ask the question. But here I am with time to speak with her.

"Do you think you two will stay together now that the summer is over?" I ask. Instant regret. I can't believe I actually asked it. My stomach starts to roller coaster as I see Manda's body language shift.

"That is the million-dollar question, Norm," Manda says, letting out a big sigh. "He is going back to school. I'm going to school. We will be hundreds of miles apart. I guess that is why they call it a summer romance." I see her shoulder slumps, and I can see that she looks tired. But also stressed, I wonder if she has stayed up all night pondering this same question."

"Do you want it to last?"

Manda looks at me and gives me a small smile. "You are full of lots of good questions tonight, aren't you, Norm?"

"I am not trying to pry. It seems that you two were happy all summer."

"It just started as fun. Sneaking off after the campers were in bed. Meeting up late at night. It was sex at the start, not a real relationship. You know what it's like." For the record, I have ZERO clue what that's like. But I nod like I do. Lies, all lies.

"But then, as the summer went on, I think it moved past that. I caught the feelings." She glances over at him, and I can tell. This has moved past being a fling. "I didn't want to be here. My father forced me to do something this summer, so the relationship started as a way to rebel against him, against this place. I have never been one to be with someone just for the sex. But I was angry." Now it's my time to feel guilty. All summer, I put Manda on a pedestal, not even looking at her as a real person with real problems. Now, I realize, she needs a friend, not a puppy in love with her.

"Do you think he has caught the feelings, too?" I ask her, moving my foot off the ottoman, giving her more space. I take one of the blankets off the couch and offer it to her. She gives me a weary smile and wraps herself in it.

"I don't know. I'd hope so. I think so. Maybe I wish so, I'd hope he is capable of something more than this." She waves her hand around the room and glances at him. "We never really talked about it." The initial hope of problems in paradise arises in me again, but this time, I push it aside to focus on what she needs.

"Why not?" I ask her. "It would seem to me that if this is

something that you really want, then you should tell him. Let him know how you feel." Again, she is silent for a spell. Deep in thought. Me? I am shocked by what is coming out of my mouth. Where is the guy waiting all summer for a chance to move in to end the relationship? As usual, I fail to take action when it is revealed.

"Maybe you're right. But does it really matter? The summer is over, right?"

"Not yet, Manda," I say to her. I point to my fake watch. "We still have tomorrow." At this, I am rewarded with a gorgeous, heart-stopping Manda smile.

"We do have tomorrow."

We both sit still. I am thinking about the time this summer when Bliss had to go back home for her parents' anniversary party, and I was here all weekend without her. Adam adopted me for the two days and wouldn't go anywhere without me. I was dragged out shopping with him, out to eat, to the movies. At the time, I was mad about it, thinking I was some pet of his. But looking at it now, I wonder if he was using me as some shield against getting closer to Manda. If he had someone else with them, he could focus on them, not allowing himself to get too close to her.

"Can I ask you a question, Manda?"

"Sure, Norm, anything."

"Your dad. Is that why you were crying the day we arrived at Camp NoTech?" Now that must have really caught her off guard. I see her collapse into herself and get a faraway look in her eyes. I panic for a minute, thinking I have offended her.

"You noticed that?"

I nod, not really wanting to say anything else that might offend her.

"You see, my parents really didn't want me home this summer. They are both doctors, real respected people in our town. I am not what they imagined for their daughter. Cheerleader, lifeguarded, not really great in school. I think they are embarrassed by me. They sent me here. I didn't even interview for the job, did you know that? All the new equipment for the kitchen, that ugly Blob at the lake? Pay for that, and your daughter can have a summer job." The tears are back, and I instantly regret saying anything. I try to still as still as I can. Looking everywhere but at her face. Especially her eyes.

"It's OK, Norm. I'm not mad at you.' I let out a giant breath I didn't even know I was holding.

"As long as I can remember, my parents have wanted nothing but for me to follow in their footsteps. I am their only child and, of course, I am supposed to be a doctor like them. Go to college where they went, med school where they met. The same life as them."

"But you don't want that?"

"Don't get me wrong. I love my parents. So thankful for everything they do for me and have done for me. But I am miserable at school. I don't want to be there. I don't want to be pre-med. I finally broke down and told them. Next thing I know, I'm stuck here, with no phone." She laughs. "I used to love my phone."

I sit there quietly. I would have never known this was inside Manda the whole summer. She seemed so perfect. So put it together. So...happy. I finally come across the perfect question ask her.

"What do you want?" I ask her. When she looks at me this time, she is smiling.

"No one has ever asked me that before. No one. I really want to be a teacher. I love kids. My favorite people when I was a child were my teachers."

"Then you should do it. Not to be rude to you or your parents, but it's your life, Manda. If teaching is what you want, then go for it."

"Oh, Norm." She sighs. "I wish it were as easy as that." She becomes withdrawn again, and I join her in the silence.

The only sound coming now is the snores of Adam on the couch, somewhere between the noise of a train and a chainsaw. We both laugh at how loud he is.

"Well, now, Norm. I told you something personal. Now you have to do the same."

I have loved you all summer, Manda. You are so beautiful.

That is what I wish I could say, but, of course, I don't. Action required, I shut down.

"My name isn't really Norm."

"What? Are you serious?" Her eyes get huge. "What are you even talking about?" I fill her in on the first day, and Adam showing up, naming me for the summer.

"Why didn't you say something?" She asks in disbelief. "We went all summer calling you the wrong name?"

"I don't know." I shrug. "At first, I thought maybe it would be cool. Having a nickname all summer, being friends with Adam. Then, after a while, it seemed kind of silly to correct it." She laughs with me, and I feel relaxed around her for the first time all summer.

"Then, what is your name?"

"My name is James." She takes this in, and a soft smile crosses her face.

"Thank you for this talk, James. It meant the world to me."

With that, she reaches up to my face and kisses me gently on the lips. A simple kiss of thanks.

It is my first kiss.

CHAPTER EIGHT

Time: 11:17 P.M.
Location: The Dining Hall Kitchen

Demarcus had spent the last hour boxing up all the unused food from the previous week. This has become his weekly ritual each Friday night. Miss Loretta buys only the best, top-tier meat, fruit, and vegetables. Which Demarcus is glad for, but man, does she buy too much.

He is finishing up the leftover meat. Steaks, brisket, and racks of ribs are carefully put in butcher paper and tied with a string. Demarcus adds those to the already big meat pile that will be picked up by the local homeless shelter tomorrow. Poor homeless people of Rock Creek, what are they going to do now that camp is over?

Standing in the brightly lit kitchen, Demarcus ties the last package. All the lights have been on ever since that first night when Cook came in late for a snack and scared her half to death. Even the little light from above the oven is left on.

Demarcus heads to the storage room and begins gathering

the leftover fruit and vegetables. Leaving enough to make a couple of meals tomorrow, he takes the boxes and starts lining them up next to the back door. It takes two or three trips to get it all. Once he is finished, he goes back into the room to do an inventory of canned and boxed goods to be donated.

He is bending over to the bottom shelf when the storage room door is slammed shut. Outside, he hears noises and movement. The room is neither small nor big by any stretch. Packed in with the food, Demarcus starts to feel walls closing in.

He moves toward the door. *BAM*. Stopping right before he grabs the knob, he hears the loud sound. Stopping himself, he listens for more sounds. He hears no more and goes to turn the doorknob.

He opens it slowly and lets the door swing open. He doesn't move, still listening for what made the sound. Nothing. He steps out of the storage room and looks around. No sign of anyone.

"Cook?" He says loudly. He waits a few minutes, hearing nothing, and he turns back to the inventory.

Demarcus starts counting the boxes of cereal they have left when the door slams shut again. Making him jump, he drops his notepad to the floor. He hears the same movement again. Without hesitating this time, he rushes to open the door.

As he comes out, he sees Andrei and Lin running out the front door carrying piles of snack cakes. He lets out a breath and laughs.

"Andrei for the win!" Demarcus shakes his head. Deciding the inventory can wait until the morning, he heads back in, turns off the light, and shuts the door. He turns around and lets out a scream.

Someone is standing right there.

"BB!" he yells. "What are you doing there?"

BB holds up a four-pack of energy drinks.

"Another all-night workout sesh?" BB nods and moves out the back door.

"Next time, don't scare me like that!" BB offers a wave as he makes his way out of the back of the kitchen.

Shaking his head, Demarcus walks to the stove to set out the pans needed for breakfast. Tomorrow will be a long day of working hard, so he's determined to give everyone a full meal to work on. He lays out each piece of cookware he will use slowly and reverently. A ritual he started when he first entered cooking competitions. He was always nervous that he would forget something he needed, so he took his time with each piece. It calms him, puts him in a trance. Preparing a meal is sacred.

Once done at the stove, he turns and lays out his knives on the island in th middle. His pride and joy. Provided for him by Miss Loretta at the beginning of the summer, he has loved working with them. Top of the line, deathly sharp, they are his summer fling. He runs his hands across them in a loving manner.

His final chore of the night is storing all the meat for the morning. He lifts the first two packages of steak and sausage and heads to the walk-in freezer. Using his feet, he unleashes the handle, and the door swings open. He shivers as the cold air comes out.

He turns sideways to make his way into the freezer. He drops the two packages and rushes back out. He makes three more trips in and out of the freezer. He has all the packages lined up neatly. Stepping back to admire the work, he feels himself back up into something poking him.

He turns. Cook's body is hanging on one of the hooks used to hold the meat. The blood has dried in her gut, but the knife is still stuck in here. Her eyes are frozen in a state of blindness and fright.

Demarcus's eyes grow huge as he realizes what he is seeing. Her body is already turning gray from the cold. Little pieces of frost hang off her intestines, coming from her gut.

Demarcus looks around the walk-in like he expects someone to be there. He finally realizes that he is in a small, cold space and runs back out the door, slamming it shut. He is shivering as he slides down the floor with his back against the door. He starts shaking his head and talking to himself.

"This can't be happening. No way that was her. Get it together, Demarcus."

He pushes himself off the ground and opens the walk-in door slowly. He peers in again and spies Cook's lifeless body. His mouth drops open. Then, he hears a noise behind him. He swings around, but no one is there. He moves back to the center table, leaving the walk-in door open.

One of his knives is missing.

Where five pristine knives were lying, there are now only four. The biggest knife, the one Demarcus likes to call Big Daddy, is gone. Then, the lights go off.

It takes a few seconds for the floodlights to come on. Demarcus is staring at the knives when a lone figure appears behind him. He senses the presence and can hear the slow breathing of the gas mask. He turns around.

Demarcus is tall, but the figure towers over him. Maybe out of instinct, maybe out of stupidity, but Demarcus throws a punch. His hand is caught. His hand is forced open and put on the table with his palm flat down.

Before he can react, a knife from the table is grabbed and stabbed through his hand deep into the wood of the table. Demarcus goes to scream, but no sound comes out. Shocked, he moves to run away, but he is stuck, his hand pinned by the knife. His other arm is grabbed and placed down the same way. In a split second, another one of Demarcus' precious knives is stabbed into it, pinning both hands to the wood. His arms are turned in a weird direction, bent back behind, and knifed through.

With both arms trapped, Demarcus is shaking. He looks up at the gas mask-wearing man before him. He is holding Big Daddy. The man takes a short look at the blade and then at Demarcus. With power, he plunges the knife into Demarcus's chest with such force that the tip of the knife goes all the way through and edges out of his back.

Demarcus's head turns and looks for someone to be there to help. There is no one. He looks down and sees the last two remaining knives. The figure picks them up and stares at Demarcus, whose head is shaking.

"No...please," he says barely above a whisper.

Before he's even done speaking, the gas-masked killer with a knife in each hand slams both of them into the sides of Demarcus's head. All five knives in a set should always be used. The killer releases the knives from his hands and gathers up Demarcus's limp and bloody body, and heads out the back door.

He leaves the kitchen in a mess.

CHAPTER NINE

"Do you mind if I squeeze in there with you? This ottoman is not comfortable." Before I can answer, Manda has joined me in the overstuffed chair. I scoot over as far as I can, but we're still very close. That my heart starts racing is an understatement.

"Besides, it is chilly in here," Manda says as she throws a blanket over us.

Now I want to make something clear right now. Again, I have never had a girlfriend. I have gone on a couple of dates to your typical school dances and such, but I have never been under a blanket with a girl like this. I know it is strange at 19 to be this inexperienced, but when you are a big guy, there is not much confidence in the female area. Besides, it is not like many people end up marrying someone they dated in high school.

Manda rests her head on my shoulder. Not really knowing what to do, I sit as still as I can. I start to think about what Bliss will think if she were to awake and see this scene. What would Adam think? Oh boy, WHAT would Adam do?

"Manda, do you think Adam is going to be mad about you sitting here with me?"

She lifts her head and giggles.

"First, he doesn't own me, so if I want to cuddle with someone, I can. And second, it's you, Norm, I mean James. You're a nice guy. He won't be threatened."

"Great. I'm a nice guy." I say, not even trying to hide the deflation in my voice.

"Don't be like that. I feel safe with you. That is all. Never underestimate how much girls love feeling safe. It's a lost quality." She pokes my nose, and with a smile, she lays her head back down.

Girls like feeling safe. Duly noted.

The wind starts to pick up outside, and we hear thunder close by. Lightning starts to flash, and rain starts to come down. The valley that Camp NoTech is settled in is famous for its summer storms. More than once this summer, we have been confined to our cabins while we waited out a giant storm.

Sometimes it can be awesome. One time, Bliss and her girls braved the squall and joined my cabin for the day. There is nothing more fun than getting a bunch of theater and art geeks together. The cramped space and cabin fever made for a creative vibe. The campers spent the day making their own plays and having a fashion show. It was one of my best memories of the summer, especially with all the boys fawning over Bliss. She was sweet and played along with them. She broke some hearts this summer.

"Yuck," Manda says. "It's going to be all hot and humid tomorrow. I do not look forward to cleaning."

BAM!

"What was that?" Manda says, sitting up.

The noise came from the back of the house. We sat still, listening.

BAM! BAM!

There it was again.

Manda throws the blanket off us, and we both stand. Adam stirs on the couch, and we stand frozen. Manda reaches over and grabs my hand.

SCRATCH

Something moves across the back window. We turn to look but see nothing there.

"Maybe that was a tree branch," I say.

"A tree branch. Yeah. That is what it is." Manda starts to move toward the back part of the Main House.

"What are you doing?" I ask.

"Don't you want to know what it is?"

"When has it ever been good to go TOWARD the noise?" But I follow Manda as she guides me by the hand. We reach the kitchen. Going slow and listening.

BAM!

The screen door slams shut. We both jump, and I find Manda in my arms. This is not the way I wanted to get close to her. I move forward through the kitchen, and I latch the screen door to the hook. I close the back door and head back to Manda.

"See. It was just the screen door," I tell her. She looks relieved. I guess she was tenser than she was letting on.

BANG! BANG! BANG! BANG! BANG!

Loud sounds race across the windows in the front of the house, and we hear people running.

"Now that wasn't the screen door," Manda says, taking my arm. She is right. I look around and grab a broom that is lying against the wall. We step back into the main room. Bliss and Adam are both still out. I'm tempted to wake them, but if it ends up being nothing, then I will be way too embarrassed.

BANG! BANG!

More sounds come from the other side of the house.

Now I am starting to get scared. I grip the handle of the broom. I head toward the front door and flick on the porch light.

CRASH!

The light instantly went out, as if someone had been waiting for it to come on. Who?

"Should we go out there?" Manda asks me. Which I wish she hadn't. The whole girls-want-to-be-safe thing is running through my head. I wish I had a phone.

"I really wish I had my phone," Manda says, reading my mind. I start to laugh.

"Is this funny?"

"Absolutely not, Manda. I tend to laugh when I get uncomfortable." Mother Nature decides that this is the perfect time to really open the heavens. You can hear the sounds like a hundred drummers on the roof. I creak the door open slowly.

Pushing the screen door open, I put the broom handle out first. I figure if there is something to attack us, maybe it would go for it first. When nothing happens, we push ourselves onto the porch.

We stand still on the porch. Rain, thunder, and lightning are going off all around us. The sky is angry. We turn around in a circle, back-to-back. Miss Loretta's main house has a wraparound porch that circles three-quarters of the house. We are right in the middle of that porch at the front door, so we have a good view from both ways.

"AHHHHHHH" Manda shouts an ear-splitting yell. I turn to where she is looking and see a figure coming around the corner, wearing a gas mask and raincoat, and holding an axe. He walks slowly toward us.

A noise comes from the other side, and we turn to look. Another figure dressed in the same is coming at us from the other side. This one is holding a machete. We are trapped.

They don't seem to be in a hurry. Manda and I twist around and around trying to find the best option.

A flash of light comes over us, and we are pulled away from the porch. We found ourselves back in the room.

"What is going on, bro?"

We turn to find Adam and Bliss awake and standing in front of us. Manda leaves me and rushes to Adam. Even in this intense moment, I feel the pain of disappointment.

"Adam, there are two people out there. I think they are trying to hurt us."

"Hurt you?" Bliss asks. Before we can answer, the door opens, and the two masked figures enter.

"Whoa, bro! You weren't kidding." Adam and I put the girls behind us. Adam takes the broom from me. He breaks it in two, leaving a sharp point at one end. We move ourselves back, ready to protect them.

The mask figure with the axe lifts his hand toward his face. With a swift move, he takes his mask off.

"Andrei got you!"

We all stand frozen. The other person with the machete takes off their mask, and Lin laughs.

"YOU JERKS!" Manda comes forward with a fire I hadn't seen all summer. She goes straight up to Andrei and punches him in the face. A mean right hook. Andrei falls to the ground with a thud, holding his face.

"Whoa! Manda!" Adam is standing over Andrei, pointing at his face. "I think you broke his nose." I hear a low moan come from Andrei, who is soaking wet on the floor. Lin stoops down to help him. She sits Andrei up. There is no blood, but you can see how his nose has been moved to the left.

"How could you do that to Andrei's nose?" Andrei yells. "Andrei's face is the money maker!"

"You're lucky I didn't do more than that," Manda says.

She charges at them again, and Adam has to grab her from behind to stop her from inflicting more damage. Manda is irate.

"Don't let her hurt Andrei," Lin says as he jumps in front of Andrei, trying to block her from attacking him further.

Bliss and I are standing off to the side. I am trying to calm down from the scare.

"Why'd you do that?" I ask.

"Yes. Why?" Manda also demands, finally done resisting Adam. Everyone is quiet. The room is tense. Lin helps Andrei up to his feet. Adam makes sure to keep a grip on Manda's arm; she is calmer but still sporting a crimson face of rage.

"I thought it would be funny, but obviously Andrei didn't think it out," he says, sounding funny with his nose all busted up. "It's the last night here. Lin and I have been planning this all summer. After Cohen told us that story, it was the perfect time."

Manda seems to be calming down some. As for me, my heart rate has returned to normal.

"We are sorry, guys," Lin says. "I really didn't think you guys would be that scared."

She looks remorseful. Can't tell about Andrei since he is still holding his nose. Lin takes him into the kitchen to get some ice, leaving the four of us standing.

"Get me out of here, Adam."

"Sure thing, babe. Norm, thanks for protecting my lady here."

He turns to me and gives me one of his bear hugs.

"Norm, my man!" Adam says. "Ready to take down two Able Dunns with a broom! I love you, bro."

"His name is not Norm." With that statement, everyone stops and looks at Manda, then at me.

"Your name is not Norm?" Bliss looks bewildered. "What does Manda mean?"

So, I'll recap the first day and my first time meeting Adam.

"You named him Norm?" Bliss is looking at Adam. "Because he is big? How rude is that?"

For his sake, Adam does look bad. I have wondered all summer if he even remembered doing this.

"Bro," he whispers. "Man, I'm sorry. I didn't think it would really catch on. I thought you would speak up, correct me, or something. But you never did, so I thought..." I really can't be mad at Adam. He is right. I could have said something at any time, but I didn't. Action required. Again.

"So, huh, what is your name?" Bliss asks me. A weird smile on her face.

"James. His name is James." Manda answered for me. With that, she hugs me tight. Adam grabs a large umbrella, and they head out into the storm. I do notice that Manda moves slows and looks to both sides of the porch before going fully out.

"Well, nice to meet you, James," Bliss says. I turn, and she holds her hand, and we shake.

"Nice to meet you, too."

"Did anything else happen while I was sleeping?"

"Sure did. I kissed Manda."

CHAPTER TEN

Time: 1:00 A.M.
Location: Camp NoTech Weight Room

BB is alone in the weight room as he is most nights. This is his time, the time to stay focused and get his workout in. The challenge during the summer, like it always is, is to be lazy. Who cares about football during June, July, and August? BB has to work hard, and nighttime is the best time.

The music is blaring. That screaming-so-you-can't-understand-a-single-word type of blaring. Pumping through the sound system that Miss Loretta has updated each year. The music fuels him. Already drenched with sweat, BB uses the music to clinch his fists and pound his chest. Working out is war.

BB downs another energy drink at full throttle, crushes the can, and tosses it to join the other three cans lying in the corner. He closes his eyes, jumping up and down, waiting for the drink to reach his veins.

Once he is fully fueled, he attacks the dumbbells with

force. One in each arm, he starts with 20 reps of both at a time, takes a break, then 20 more. Grunts escape with each pull upward. This is war. BB uses the anger of the music to increase the reps faster and faster. The sanctuary of the weight room is where he goes to church.

He drops the dumbbells down and screams. BB is feeling good. Real good. He could go all night. He is unstoppable. He grabs the jump rope off the wall, counting down from five. On his side, he attacks the rope: 25 jumps, 50 jumps, 100 jumps. He won't stop. He can't stop. This is war. Like the commercial says, "Somewhere, someone is working harder than you." More and more sweat is dripping off him. It is getting in his eyes, but he doesn't care. He squints them shut and keeps going. Three hundred jumps.

Another primal scream escapes as he reaches 500 jumps. He throws the rope down and flexes. BB is unstoppable tonight. There is no time for rest. The music kicks into another new song. This one is even faster, even angrier. BB looks around for the next victim. He notices the bench press. He looks at it like a lion looks at its prey. BB is hungry.

He puts on his gloves and settles himself onto the bench. Three hundred and fifty pounds. He attacks it. He comes down and back up with ease. This is nothing. He gets up and adds more weight. Four hundred pounds. Back on the bench, he grips the bar and lifts. Down and up again. There is nothing stopping him tonight. He flexes in the head-to-floor mirrors that serve as walls. His tight black shirt blends in with his skin, with the words ATECH in all white across the shirt. He can't wait to get back on the field!

He adds even more weight. Five hundred pounds. Sometimes you need a challenge.

He lays back on the bench. He focuses on the bar, telling himself that no one is the boss. He is my boss. He grips the bar and rises. Now this is more like it. A true challenge for the lion. He holds it steady. All the lessons and warnings athletes are given since middle school about lifting alone are flashing through his mind. Always have a partner. Never lift alone. He needs no one.

Bringing the bar down slowly, his grip is growing weaker. He struggles to get it down. Once it comes there, he screams, pushes his back up, and sets it in the holder. Five hundred pounds. BB lets out another yell, cupping his hands around his mouth. He hops off the bench. He did it. The lion killed the prey.

BB, with his eyes closed, is still pulsing with energy. His brain is moving at a million miles an hour. He is in the zone.

The music stops.

The silence that is left is just as loud. He opens his eyes and looks around. Why did the music stop? He starts to move toward the sound system, and when he gets closer, the music kicks back on.

BB grabs his ears. A pained scream escapes. He drops to one knee. The energy drink is wearing off. The music is so loud. Rubbing his eyes, he stands back up and opens them, sweat stinging his sight.

Someone is standing in front of him.

BB does a double-take. Maybe it's the fuel of the drink or the adrenaline wearing off, but it seems this guy is wearing a gas mask. In his right hand, he is holding one of the weight bars. BB glances down and sees the weights on the floor.

When he looks back up, the gas-masked person swings the bar against the side of BB's head. It hurts him hard, and he stumbles to the side. Blood starts to come out of this ear. But he doesn't go down. The figure swings again, this time hitting BB on his side, taking out all his ribs at once.

BB drops to one knee, clutching his side. He tries his hardest to get back up. The figure stands there looking down at him. His head kind of glances to one side as if saying, "This one is tough." BB rises back to his feet. He stands erect and looks at the figure before him.

The music is still as blaring as BB charges forward, spearing the man into the full-length glass that adorns the side of the wall. Glass shatters everywhere. BB falls to the ground as the figure with the gas mask doesn't budge at all.

Blood is running down BB's arms from broken glass. He stands upright as another blow from the bar crashes down on the back of his head. This blow leaves BB dazed and barely moving. Another blow from the bar puts him on the ground. He is still trying to move around, rustling along a floor of sweat, glass, and blood.

BB rolls over on his back. The man leans over him. He picks up BB and drags him back to the weight bench, where just earlier, BB was the dominator. Not anymore. The man lifts BB like it is a feather and plops it back on the bench, facing the ceiling.

The bar is placed on BB's neck and is pressed down hard. The flesh starts to rip, and his neck is torn. He keeps pushing down, pulling the neck farther away from the body. Gargling sounds escape from BB. Blood is gushing all over the hands on the bar. With a superhuman grunt, he pushes one final time, ripping BB's head clear off his body. It makes a wet plop on the floor.

CHAPTER ELEVEN

"What do you mean you kissed Manda?"

I lean back, putting my head behind my head, and give Bliss a sly smile, keeping the details to myself. A true smuggler kissing a princess.

"No, you don't, Han Solo me!" she says, throwing a pillow at me. I enjoy what may be the only chance I will ever have to be the cocky boy. The one who kissed the hot chick. Oh, how it would drive Bliss crazy to leave her in the dark.

But that isn't me.

"Well, it's more like she kissed me." Bliss grabs my face and shakes it in her hands.

"She kissed *you*??" Bliss looks crazed, letting go of my face. Bewildered. I chuckle and shrug my shoulders again.

"I guess she wanted some of this all summer," I say. But before I finish the sentence, I am laughing. She hits me on the arm. I fill her in on the talk Manda and I had, leaving out the part about her crying the first day. Bliss gets a huge smile on her face.

"Manda is right, by the way," Bliss says.

"Really? About what?"

"Girls want to feel safe. Girls want to be protected. They want to know more than anything that you will protect them. They need that assurance." She sits there smiling at me. Proud.

"Good for you, James," she says. "You got to kiss the girl."

"So, about the whole name thing..." I start to say to her. I really don't want her to think that I was trying to hide anything from her. I can't do anything that would jeopardize the relationship I have with Bliss.

"No, I get it. It's summer. You have the chance to be someone different here. Besides, if you didn't like any of us, then when we leave, we wouldn't even know your name." I laughed really loud.

"That is a good point. I could leave here, and you all would be searching for Norm, but Norm has vanished, drifting off into the night." I float my fingers along the air. "A true man of mystery." She laughs with me. "I still should have told you." She shrugs it off.

"UGH! Andrei is going to die!"

"Really? Again?" Lin and Andrei make their way back out of the kitchen. Andrei has a bag of ice on his face and is being led by the hand across the room. He resembles a toddler being led by his mother. It actually fits their relationship. Lin has been mothering Andrei all summer.

"Leave Andrei alone. I am in pain." He collapses onto one of the couches.

"You deserve it," Bliss says. I can see that she is still angry over what happened and how much it upset Manda. It is a wonder that Bliss herself doesn't go and punch Andrei again.

"Let it go, Bliss. Andrei is sorry. What else do you want?" Andrei sounds like a muffled voice coming over the PA system in a grocery store. "Let's get out of here, Lin. Andrei needs to lie down."

Without waiting for a response, Andrei storms out the

front door. Lin sticks around for a bit. I can tell she is struggling with what to say next.

"I am sorry. It went too far," she says. "I do love that man, but sometimes I let him get out of control. I should have seen that it was too far. But you know him, when he is hooked on an idea... Well, you can't stop him." We both nod at her, and she heads out.

Bliss and I take some time and clean up the main room of the Main House. We shut down the karaoke machine and box it up. We each grab a trash bag and start moving around the room collecting food and cups. Another downfall of being the sober one, you are the one who cleans up. I count 14 beer bottles by the chair BB was sitting in and wonder how he is even standing.

We make sure to take our time and make everything nice for when Miss Loretta returns. She does not like messes.

"What do we do with this axe and machete?" I ask Bliss. "Now that is a sentence I never thought I would say."

"Prop them up against the wall. We can go ask Cohen where he wants them." I move them to the far, marveling at how heavy they are. I don't know how Lin was even able to carry one.

The rain has finally stopped for the moment. We take the bags out to the dumpster and make our way over to Cohen. There is a nice wooden walkway that weaves throughout the camp. It has lamp posts every four feet. Miss Loretta is a big fan of *The Lion, the Witch, and the Wardrobe*, so the lamps were expensively made. Bliss links her arm into mine.

"Now keep me safe," she says.

"Always."

Since it is the middle of the night, the air is cool after the rain. I make a mental note to enjoy this walk since it may be the last stroll we get together this summer.

"I wouldn't have left without telling you my real name."

"I know," Bliss says.

We make our way down the path, arm in arm. The campground is wonderful at night. Even when the campers were here, this was the most enjoyable time. Miss Loretta likes to talk all the time about the big divorce that led to the building of camp. After going through a horrendous event, she wanted a magical place where she was happy everywhere she went and looked.

"Technology is the real mistress in my marriage," she says. "My husband had so many avenues with which to cheat on me. Phones, tablets, computers, and smart watches. He used them all."

Her despising of all things modern led her to establish Camp NoTech. She enjoys being cut off. She loves the solitude, and she taught us all summer her belief that this generation needs to learn the dangers of technology. But they can only understand that if they are cut off from it. She encourages parents who are considering the camp to send their child for at least two weeks. Or like Hitts, a month. Must have been a big divorce settlement. Miss Loretta likes nice things.

We hear a door bang, and we look to our left.

"You think that came from Cohen's place?" I ask. Cohen lives in a small cabin a little off from the rest of the camp. We look and see lights still coming from his windows.

"Why in the world is he still up?" Bliss says, guiding us off the walkway onto the dirt path. We make our way up toward the cabin. She unhooks her arms from mine and holds one finger up to her mouth, telling me to be quiet. Now, Cohen may be old and a little off, but I don't find it odd that he is up late on the last night of camp. He lives in the nearby town of Rock Creek but stays here during the summer and the weekends when Miss Loretta holds "Tech-Detox" weekends. He must be packing up to move back home.

THUMP!

A noise escapes from inside the cabin, and we stop in our tracks. The wind is starting to pick up again, and I see lightning off in the distance.

"What are you going to do? Walk to the door and knock? It's 2 in the morning," I whisper to Bliss. She puts her finger back up to her mouth and then uses it to point to the side of the house. We creep around to the side and peer into the window.

Cohen is covered in blood.

It doesn't seem to me that he is bleeding; therefore, the blood must not be his. The small man is still dressed in his normal work attire, but the overalls are stained red. He leaves the room, and we wait. We heard some noises and a few grunts, and he returns, dragging something large into the living room. It is wrapped in a white sheet and is trailing blood behind it.

Bliss gasps and grabs my hand. What a weird night. Girls keep grabbing my hand.

He drags the body, at least it looks like a body, all the way through the living room, headed to the kitchen. We move down to the next window and wait to see where he is headed.

SNAP!

I step on a stick, and Cohen drops the package. He looks right at us. We know he sees us, so we take off back toward the front of the house.

The porch light flicks on, and we are caught.

CHAPTER TWELVE

Time: 2:51 A.M.
Location: Cabin 9

Lin Ai is exhausted. Why did she ever let herself be talked into that plan by Andrei? Plopping down on her bed, she covers herself up and tries to go to sleep. She is restless despite the comfortable bed.

Miss Loretta spared no expense on the cabins. It should be called "Glamp NoTech." Each cabin is wooden, and five beds line each wall of the room. There is one big bathroom that holds four private showers and four private stalls. Even more important to girls, there are four sinks, but even that is not enough. Fighting is a morning ritual.

In front of the bathroom wall sits a gas fireplace. Off to one corner is the counselor's space. Lin has enjoyed a queen bed to herself all summer with a private bathroom. She also enjoys having her own closet, unlike campers, who have trunks at the end of their beds. The closet is where Lin goes after getting out of bed. Opening the door, she pushes aside all her clothes and bends down to lift part of the floor.

Under the floor, she reaches down and pulls out a black case. Putting the floor back down, she closes the closet door. She unzips the case and pulls out a sleek silver laptop. Even though it is the last night of camp, she is still nervous that she will get caught. With one last peek outside into the main room, she boots up the laptop. The glow lights up the small space, and Lin basks in it like a giant lightning bug.

The secret laptop has been Lin's saving grace this summer. The solitude of the closet, combined with the risk of being caught, has helped her survive the no-technology rule. While the internet is a luxury only given once a week when they all go into town on Saturday, she can still enjoy her favorite game.

"Rapture" is a puzzle game that requires the player to dodge attackers and survive as long as possible. Each Saturday, Lin uploads her results to the world leaderboard. Currently number 2 in the world, Lin spends hours each night in the closet trying to get better. She makes sure the laptop is plugged into the battery pack she charges when the cabin is empty. She closes her eyes and loads the game.

The Rapture title screen pops up, and Lin exhales. She focuses on herself. Starting at level 1, it isn't until level 30 or higher that Lin feels anything close to a challenge. She is closing on level 60 when she hears someone out in the cabin. Pausing the game, she closes the laptop and puts it back in the bag. She peeks out of the closet door.

Poking her head out a little further, she listens.

"Andrei, is that you?" No answer.

She shuts the closet door and reopens the laptop. She is about to start when she hears the noise again. She opens the door, figuring that if it is Miss Loretta, she will only be upset for one night. But again, there is no one there. She places the laptop down and moves out of the closet.

Across the room, she sees that the main door is open. Lin

makes her way over, opens the screen door, and looks outside. She sees some lightning off in the distance. The storm is circling back for round two. Lin can already see some drops coming down. She steps back inside, closing both doors. Maybe the noise she heard was from the door swinging open.

She heads back to the closet when she notices the main bathroom lights are on. They were not on earlier. Taking a longing glance at the closet, she instead turns toward the bathroom. Maybe they were on, and she didn't notice.

Walking into the bathroom, she doesn't notice anything at first. She glances around the corner, and all the private stalls are closed except the last one. Heading down the row, she sees a trail of red liquid on the floor. She pushes past the door and looks into the stall.

BB's headless body is sitting in the stall.

Lin screams and backs away. She takes off, running past the other stalls and back out the door.

She runs into the man wearing the gas mask.

She hits him like a wall, and it knocks her to the floor. She looks up in time to see the man grab her by the hair and throw her across the room. She bangs off the wall and falls. He is right on top of her. Picking her up again, he repeats the same motion. She slams through a window and onto the ground below. The rain has started pouring again.

Lin is dazed. Rolling to one side, she tries to get up. She crawls back in front of the cabin. Clawing at the ground, she tries to move away from the cabin.

The man follows her, grabs her by the hair again, and drags her back to the cabin. A scream escapes from Lin as the door shuts. Once again, she is tossed across the room. Landing on her bed, she bounces on the floor in front of the closet. She drags herself in and closes the door.

Lin's breaths are rapid as she tries to hide herself in the back corner behind the clothes. She hears steps coming toward her. She hears nothing for a few moments, and she is praying that he is gone.

He isn't.

A hand busts through the door, causing Lin to scream again. Again and again, breaking all the wood apart. Finally, the whole door is ripped off the hinges and tossed away. Lin scrambles over to the other end of the closet and grabs her closed laptop.

She stands to face the masked man.

He pauses.

Lin attacks. She hits the man in the face with the laptop over and over again. She finally collapses in exhaustion. The effect is nothing to him.

The figure reaches down and takes the laptop. Lin, on her knees, looks up, begging for him. "No."

With one powerful swing, the man crashes the laptop across Lin's face. Blood is splattered as she collapses. Dead. He pushes her back into the closet, tosses the laptop on top of her, and closes the door.

CHAPTER THIRTEEN

Cohen is out on the porch, bloody overalls and all, staring at us. All summer, I would never once have pegged Cohen as scary. Maybe because he is so short or the fact that he is always helping me fix things, he's never given off the covered-in-blood, axe murderer vibe.

But he is now.

"What are you two doing out here?" He snarls at us. "Why are you looking in my window at this time of night?" He starts toward us, and we back away. I stand in front of Bliss.

"We saw your light on," I say, offering back to him.

"So? No crime in having my light on, is there?" He snaps back. I don't like this side of Cohen. The sweet and wise-natured man that I worked with all summer is not present here.

"No," I stammer. "But we wanted to ask you something. Since the lights were on, we thought you were still up."

"Wanted to ask me something? It couldn't wait until morning?"

"It could have, I guess." Bliss starts to pull at me, leading us away.

"Come on, Norm. Let's get out of here." I turn to go with her.

"NO!" Cohen yells. It stops us dead in our tracks. He is now standing on the edge of the porch. The rain starts to fall again. We hear a scream in the distance.

"Get back here," he orders. Bliss and I look at each other. Our hesitancy must have irked Cohen. "RIGHT NOW!" he screams. We stand a few seconds longer in the rain before heading back toward him. He backs up, and we climb the steps. We are out of the rain, but I have a feeling that we have stepped into something else.

"Tell me what you saw when you looked in the window," Cohen asks.

"We didn't see anything," Bliss says. "Nothing."

"Nothing," I say in agreement.

Cohen takes a step toward us. He looks at us. A long look.

"Come inside." No explanation. He turns around and heads back inside.

I don't move, and Bliss doesn't move.

"Yeah, I really don't want to go in there," I say to her. I feel her tense up next to me, confirming that she feels the same way. To be honest, what does one do in this type of situation? You have a man covered in blood dragging what appears to be a body through his house. He has now ordered you in.

"In here now," we hear Cohen say from inside the living room.

"If anything starts to happen, I want you to run," I tell Bliss. I have thought about this situation many times. I am a big guy. I am very slow, and I can't run for very long. I always knew I would be the sacrifice.

"Enough of that talk. I am sure there is a reasonable

explanation for all this." If she has thought this a perfectly reasonable explanation, she doesn't share it. My stomach is in turmoil as we enter the cabin.

The first thing I notice as I walk in is that the blood trail we already knew was there is that it runs the length of the wooden floor and into the kitchen. I have been in Cohen's cabin before. It is sparse. A chair in one corner and a book-shelf along the wall. I have borrowed a few titles this summer. A small table.

Cohen is standing in the archway that separates the two rooms with his back to us. I look past him and see the white bundle on the kitchen floor. The contrast between the brightness of the kitchen melding into the darkness of the living room makes one feel like Cohen is standing between two worlds.

"We saw you dragging the body across the floor," Bliss tells him. I see Cohen tense up, clenching his fists. But he relaxes and turns toward us.

"You think it is a body?"

"It looks like one," Bliss replies. Cohen reaches up, as if to rub his eyes, but at the last moment, he realizes they are covered in blood. Instead, he shakes his head and looks back at us. He looks tired.

"So, that is what you two concluded? You see me dragging something through my house late at night. It leaves this blood trail all the way in there. You see a white bundle, stained in blood. Not to mention that I stand here before you covered in blood myself." He pauses. "So, your conclusion is a dead body. Your brain settles on the logic that I must have killed someone."

"No one said anything about you killing someone," I say. Bliss and I both jump as a clap of thunder rips through the cabin. Cohen doesn't move.

"But you think there is a body in there." He says, nodding back toward the kitchen.

"So, that's not a body?" Bliss asks.

"No. It's a body. But I didn't kill anyone."

We all three stand there in silence. The only thing I notice is the rain and my heart racing. I wonder what comes next.

"Who is that in there, Cohen?" Bliss asks. I see Cohen drop his head.

"Now, before I tell you what I am about to tell you, I need you both to trust me." The earnestness in his voice gives me pause. What IS in the kitchen?

"Cohen, what is going on?" Bliss breaks away from me and heads toward him. I grab her hand and bring her back. She shakes away from me.

"Bliss, what are you doing?" She ignores me. As she gets close to Cohen, he looks up at her but doesn't move. Bliss touches his arm as she moves past him into the kitchen. It was a slight touch. One to convey calm. I admire her bravery.

I, too, start to cross the room. Cohen moves out of my way and slumps into the old chair. I follow Bliss into the kitchen, where she is standing by the bundle. I move to stand by her.

"Do we look to see what it is?" I ask.

"You mean WHO it is?" Bliss replies.

Bliss bends down and starts unwrapping. It's bound tight, and seeing it up close, you can tell that the person or thing in it is quite big. I bend to help her with the process. I despise blood, but there is no way not to get blood on my hands as I do this. We struggle and finally rip away the final layer.

Cook is lying there in blood.

CHAPTER FOURTEEN

Time: 3:23 A.M.
Location: Cabin 1

Manda and Adam are sitting on the bench outside the cabin. Adam has his arm around Manda, trying to keep her warm. She is still shaken up from the encounter with Andrei.

"It's OK, babe. Don't even worry about Andrei."

"That's easy for you to say, Adam. You were drunk and passed out on the couch. You weren't out there with us." She stiffens in his arms.

"I'm sorry. I drank too much. I should have been awake."

"Yes, you should have." Adam pulls her closer and starts snuggling her neck. He moves her hair out of the way and starts to kiss her neck.

"Are you kidding me?" Manda says, standing up. "After all that, you expect me to do that tonight?'

"I said I was sorry," he says, standing up. "What more do you want me to say?"

"How about not getting completely wasted in the first

place? How about you don't pass out for once? How about you stay awake so when a psycho pretends to be another psycho, you are there for me. For me and Norm."

"His name isn't Norm." That is the final straw. Manda throws up her hands. Pushing him aside, she moves into the cabin.

"And what is that all about?" she yells, turning back toward him. "Bro! You're enormous! I'm going to call you Norm! How could you do that to him?"

Adam doesn't respond. He looks like a cross between shame, anger, and frustration.

"I didn't mean it to be something like this. I told him I was sorry."

"You think that matters to him? He spent all summer with a name that was made up because of his size. If he were black, would you have said anything like that to him?"

"Of course not! I'm not one to say something to someone about their race."

"Oh, but is it OK to make fun of his size? How is that any different?"

"I...uh..." Adam struggles for the words. "I am sorry. I really am. It was stupid of me."

"It sure was." With that, Manda walks off, headed toward the back of the cabin. She stops and comes charging back. Adam throws up his hands to block his face.

"Don't hit me!"

"I'm not going to hit you, but I need you to look at me." She stands as tall as she can, her tiny frame trying to make an impact next to Adam.

"Sure," he says, looking at her.

"What are we doing here, Adam?" She makes a motion with her hands symbolizing the "we."

"What do you mean? It's late. We are soaked. We need to get some sleep before tomorrow."

"Not right this second," she says, groaning. "I mean us, you and me, Adam and Manda. The summer is done, bro. What is going to happen to us?" Adam is staring at her, confused by what she is saying.

"To us?" he asks.

"Yes. To us. Are we anything after tomorrow? Or do we return to school and forget all about our summer?" The question is met with a long pause. He starts to look everywhere but at Manda.

"I don't know."

"You don't know?" Manda gasps. " Great. Well, I guess that gives me my answer, doesn't it?" She starts to move away, but Adam grabs her to bring her back to him.

"I'm serious. I don't know. We never talked about it." He pleads. "What do you want? I have no clue where you stand." Manda shakes his hand off her, but is starting to calm down.

"What do you want?" she asks back.

"I mean, I really loved hanging out with you this summer. You are so cute, and man, the sex, I mean the sex is like... WOW!"

"Well, thanks, I guess," Manda says, letting out a small chuckle.

"I guess I was waiting for you to say something. I mean, you are the smart one in this relationship, not me." When Adam says this, Manda smiles.

"OK, Adam. Here is what I think. I like you. I really do. Sometime this summer, in the midst of all the WOW sex, I kind of started to feel more for you. I guess I was hoping you would say something, too. So, I would be spared any embarrassment if you didn't feel the same way."

"Well, Manda," Adam says, pulling her closer to him. "Let me end that mystery now. I feel the same way."

"You do?"

"Sure thing, bro." He kisses her. "Camp ends tomorrow. Why don't we make it official?"

"Official, how?"

"Manda. Will you be my girlfriend?" he says with a chuckle.

"Yes, I will. But just one thing."

"Anything."

"Don't call me bro before you kiss me." They both laugh.

"Sure thing."

"And apologize to James. I mean, *really* apologize. He is a good guy."

"I will. I promise."

"Ok." She pushes off Adam. 'Shower time."

"You got it." Adam starts to peel off his shirt, and Manda stops him.

"No, Romeo. By myself."

"Well, that's no fun." She leaves Adam standing there with a puppy-dog look on his face.

CHAPTER FIFTEEN

"Oh, my god," Bliss says, backing away from the body.

I am too stunned to move. I am still clutching the white sheet, blood squeezing through my fingers. What am I seeing? This is a dead body. I have never seen a dead body before. It reminds me of that movie from the '80s that my dad made me watch. In it, a group of friends embarks to see a dead body. I remember some of it. The only thing that stuck with me is that the fat guy in it pukes all over everyone.

But this is no movie. Cook is lying here. Right here in Cohen's kitchen. How did she get here? What happened to her? She looks like an animal clawed her stomach. And the smell? Oh my goodness, the smell.

It's Bliss who moves first. She moves me back. Taking the sheet from my hand, she places it back over Cook's face. We both stand there for a good five minutes. Neither of us speaks. Again, the rain and my heartbeat are all I hear.

"I didn't kill her." Cohen's voice breaks the trance that we are in. We turn, and he is standing at the edge of the kitchen. I am amazed at where I am right now. Right between a dead body and a man covered in blood, claiming that he didn't kill said dead body. Stuck between a rock and a dead body. With that thought, I let out a chuckle.

"What is funny?" Bliss says, looking at me. If looks could kill, there would be another dead body in here.

"Nothing. I laugh when I'm nervous." If I ever had a time to feel nervous, it is right now.

"Why don't you two clean up?" Cohen says, moving back into the living room.

Bliss and I head over to the sink and turn on the water. We let it warm up while we look for towels to use. I find a roll of paper towels under the sink. We spend the next few moments scrubbing the blood off our arms and hands. I can't help but stare down at the blood as it comes off and goes down the drain. That is Cook's blood, I think.

I finish up and see Bliss staring back at the body.

"What are we going to do?" I whisper to her.

"What do you mean?" she whispers back. I steal a glance toward the living room.

"What do I mean? There is a dead body right here! We need to call the cops or something." Bliss stands there and doesn't say anything at first.

"You're right," she says. "But let's hear what Cohen has to say first. Perhaps this can be explained."

"Be explained? She is dead."

"I know Norm, I mean James, and she is dead," Bliss says, motioning with her hands. "She is lying right there...dead. Talking to Cohen isn't going to make her any more dead. Let's listen to him, and I promise we will call the police. Deal?"

I don't like it. I don't like it all. If television and movies have taught me anything, it's that if you find a dead body, you call the police. If you don't, bad things happen. But I feel like I have no choice.

"Deal," I say reluctantly.

Cohen is back in his chair, drinking something brown from a glass, when we come back into the room. There isn't anywhere else to sit, and the floor is out of the question. It is covered in blood. So, we stand.

"Cohen?" Bliss says. "What happened?"

Cohen says nothing. He takes a long drink.

"I went to the dining hall," he begins. "I was hungry. I knew that Demarcus would have put up all the food for tomorrow's pick up, but I figured I could still find something to eat." He takes another drink. He looks pale.

"There is nothing strange about that, I tell you. I do this often. Miss Loretta, Cook, and Demarcus all know I go in sometimes and get something to eat. I didn't finish my food earlier tonight. I was hungry. That is all. Hungry..." He trails off, looking at nothing. Another drink goes down.

"I went to the kitchen and flicked on the light." He pauses. He is seeing something in his mind that we can't.

"There was blood everywhere. All over the kitchen. It looked like something had been slaughtered. I should have been scared. Maybe I should have run away. But I didn't. I saw the trail of blood leading out of the back door and more trailing toward the walk-in freezer." He closes his eyes and rubs them. I don't think he remembered that there was blood on them. It leaves him looking like a cannibal that you see in those documentaries.

"I know now I should have just left. I should have come back here, grabbed my keys, and headed to the Main House and used the landline. But I didn't."

"You looked in the freezer," Bliss says.

"I did," Cohen says, nodding. "I saw Cook just hanging there. She was blue and frozen from being in there."

"Why did you bring her back here?" I ask.

"I don't know. I panicked. I wanted to hide the body and clean up the mess. But as I took her down and dragged her back here, she started to, I don't know, thaw out? The blood was spreading everywhere. When I got here, I ran inside and grabbed a sheet from my bed." He pauses. "If this got out, that would be the end of the camp. Miss Loretta is in enough trouble as it is. A murder is the last thing she needs."

"What do you mean, Miss Loretta is in trouble?" I ask. Now it looks like there is another secret we are about to get out of Cohen tonight. He twists and turns in his chair, looking uneasy.

"Cohen. What is going on with Camp NoTech?" Bliss asks again.

"Miss Loretta is broke. Or going broke. Close to broke. I really don't know. I can't get a straight answer out of her. All I know is that there is financial trouble. That is why she disappears every weekend. She is trying to get donors for the camp."

"You mean she doesn't have a boyfriend?" I ask.

"A boyfriend?" Cohen laughs at this. "Miss Loretta doesn't like boyfriends if you get my drift." I look at Bliss. Did she know this?

"Yes, I knew." She interprets my look. "It isn't my place to reveal that information."

"You two aren't..." I say.

"God, no!" she says, slapping me.

"Not that there is anything wrong..."

"No, James." She snaps at me. End of discussion.

"James?" Cohen asks.

"Long story," I say. "Why did you bring the body here?"

"I wanted to hide it," Cohen says, taking another drink. "I figured I would hide it, clean up the mess, and then dispose of it after everyone left for the summer."

"What in the world gives you the right to dispose of her body?" Bliss says.

But we don't get an answer. A scream pierces through the storm.

CHAPTER SIXTEEN

Time: 3:55 A.M.
Location: Cabin 1

Manda takes her time enjoying the shower. To his credit, Adam has only tried to get in three times. But she has kept this moment for herself. She needed the time to think.

"He likes me, too." A smile escapes her face. Maybe this summer wasn't a waste after all. She continues to enjoy the hot water and hears Adam get in the stall next to hers. Sure enough, a few seconds later, his singing starts up. Adam knows every word to every song made by every boy band ever.

Her thoughts ran back to early this summer when she first started to think more of him. It was the third week of camp, the fourth that they had all been there, and the counselors decided to hold a lip sync battle. It was the guys against the girls. There were two rounds, and the losers had to do all the dish duty for the entire week. She, Bliss, Belle, and Lin were determined not to lose.

They rehearsed all day Sunday. The boys were locked away doing the same. The performance was going to be the first thing at the beginning of camp, right after the ritual where the campers give up their phones. She laughs as she remembers Miss Loretta egging on each group, offering a big bonus for whatever team won. It was going to be a battle in every sense of the word.

The night came, and all 100 campers were seated in the amphitheater. They weren't in a good mood since they had all just lost their phones for five days. Five whole days! The horror. She and the other girls were nervous backstage as they waited for the boys to go first. They all snuck around to the side of the stage to watch.

The boys' first round was all of them dressed up in drag like the Spice Girls. Andrei—who else?—took the lead as they sing and dance. Adam was in the background for most of this one. It seemed like he wasn't into the lip sync thing and was acting too cool. NO, he was playing coy until the next round. But before that, it was the girls' turn.

The girls worked out a whole routine to the world-famous "Baby Got Back" song. Since none of the girls were blessed with tremendous backsides, they added some padding to it. The campers loved it. Being that Lin knew every word to the song, it was phenomenal. There was a short break before the girls went first to start round two.

The girls kicked down the house with the classic song "MmmBop." There was no way the boys could beat that. But again, the girls underestimated Adam. They had all witnessed his love for boy bands during the first few weeks, as he would always sing wherever he was. But this was about to go to a whole different level.

The guys were all dressed in matching white dress shirts and blue jeans. Adam started the song off and unbuttoned his shirt, making all the girl campers shriek. Even the girl counselors were all happy. Once he took the shirt off, well, long story short, the boys won.

Easily.

Manda turns off the shower and dries off. She had been keeping a change of clothes in Cabin 1 since the second week. She got them out and got dressed. Adam was still singing in the shower; the temptation to join him was there, but she was enjoying her time with her thoughts. She went and waited for him in his bed.

She heard Adam finish up and make his way out. She pretended to sleep, knowing that any second he would get her attention. "Being with" Adam is going to be exhausting. He is sometimes like a little puppy. You need to play with him every once in a while, or he gets lonesome.

"Warning," Adam says. Manda glances one eye open, and Adam is standing, wearing nothing but a towel. "I am naked under this towel. This is your final warning."

"I'm way too tired for that, Adam." She rolls over and hopes Adam takes the hint. Looking disappointed, Adam makes his way back into the bathroom. Poor little puppy. Closing her eyes again, Manda tries to sleep. She is not looking forward to all the work that has to start in the next few hours.

She must have fallen asleep for a bit because the next thing she is jolting awake from a sound coming from outside the window by her. She shakes it off as a dream and tries to go back to sleep.

THUMP.

There it is again. She sits up and listens.

THUMP.

There it is again. It sounds like someone is banging against the back of the cabin. She turns toward where she thinks the noise is coming from, but nothing.

"Adam?" Manda calls out, but no answer.

THUMP.

The sound comes again. This time closer, and Manda could hear the movement outside. The rain was still coming down, so there is nothing showing through the curtains. That is, until the lightning hits. The flash lasts long enough for Manda to see a huge figure standing right outside the window.

She clasps her hand over her mouth to try to stop the scream that wants to escape. Who is that? She hears the movement outside again. Another flash of lightning, and the figure is now at the next window. Manda crawls off the bed and moves across the room. If he is trying to get into the cabin, she can lock the door before he gets there.

Another flash of lightning, and the person has moved on to the next window. They are definitely moving toward the front. Even if it is Andrei trying to pull another scare on us, she isn't about to let him in or get away with it.

She reaches the door and locks it. She even turns the handle to make sure it locks. Turning the lock again, she feels satisfied. She backs away slowly. Scanning the room, she notices some sports equipment. She takes a metal bat in her hand. She grips it tight and braces for a fight.

"Bro, what are you doing?"

Manda jumps, turns, and raises the bat, ready to take out someone.

"Whoa, babe!" Adam jumps back. "Whoa, whoa. Take it easy."

"There is someone out there, Adam," Manda hisses at him. Adam stares at her and then looks toward the door.

"What? Who?" He tries to take the bat from Manda, but she has a death grip on it.

THUMP.

A sound comes again. Whoever is out there is now in

front of the house. Adam stops cold. He hears the walking outside now.

"Give me the bat, Manda."

This time, Manda hands over the bat without objection. They both stand there waiting. Adam has the bat gripped and is holding up, ready to swing. Whoever is out there is taking their sweet time. Adam pushes Manda behind him. He sets his stance, forearms tight as he grips the bat.

But right then, a scream echoes through the camp.

Adam and Manda hear a loud noise in front, a sound like running away.

Another scream escapes into the night.

"We need to go out there," Adam says.

CHAPTER SEVENTEEN

I hear a second scream come through the storm. I look at Bliss and Cohen.

"What was that?" I ask.

"No clue," Bliss replies. "But it doesn't sound good." She starts to head to the door. She opens it and is listening hard. But all we can hear is the rain on the roof of the porch. Cohen and I join her, looking out into the night.

A third and more extreme scream escapes. We all three take off into the rain, running down the path toward the cabins. As usual, I am lagging behind. Running is not my strength. Bliss is swift like a doe, and for his age, Cohen is fast. I notice that Manda and Adam are coming out of Cabin 1. Adam is carrying a metal bat. It may be the best idea he has ever had.

The others meet up in the gazebo that sits in the middle of the walkway. I show up a few seconds later, out of breath. We all stand under the lighted gazebo in a circle with our backs toward each other. We are all watching and waiting to see or hear what is happening.

I hear another scream, and we all turn to see Andrei running out of Cabin 9. Lin's cabin.

"Andrei!" Manda yells. He sees us and runs toward the gazebo. He looks deathly afraid. He is at top speed as he makes his way to us. He stumbles, does a roll, and backs up again all in one swoop. He is out of breath when he enters the gazebo. Collapsing on the ground, we all bend down to check on him.

"What's wrong, Andrei?" Bliss asks first, but soon we are all speaking on top of each other.

"What's in the cabin?"

"Are you hurt?"

"I have a bat, bro. Tell me what to do!"

Andrei is shaking so hard we can't get him to calm down. He keeps pointing to the cabin and crying. Bliss holds him close to her chest, trying to get him to relax, soothing him like a mother would a hurt child. I have never seen Andrei like this. No one has. The mascara he wears every day is all smooshed and running. It makes him look like a Goth raccoon. I let out a chuckle.

"NOT the right time," Bliss says, looking at me. "Andrei, I need you to calm down. You need to tell us what is wrong. What happened in the cabin?"

"Is Lin alright, son?" Cohen says. Andrei takes one look at him, still covered in blood, dried blood on his face, and loses it. He screams again, and I realize why we can hear him through the rain pouring. He tries to back away from Cohen but ends up knocking over Bliss. He backs all the way up to the wall of the shelter.

"Andrei!" Bliss orders. "Cohen is OK. He hasn't done anything. What is in the cabin?" Andrei looks down again, shaking his head frantically.

"She's dead. She's dead," he keeps repeating over and over.

"Who is dead?" Bliss says and reaches for his arm.

"LIN!" he shouts. Thunder and lightning hit at that moment, making us all jump again.

"Whoa, bro. What do you mean she is dead?" Adam says in disbelief.

"I mean, she is dead. In the closet. In the closet! She is dead!" He goes back to shaking again. He stops and looks at Cohen. "Did you do this?" he screams. Cohen is taken aback, but his face remains calm.

"I did not do this, Andrei," he says in a soft voice. I can barely hear him. "But it is very important that you tell me exactly what is up there." Andrei shakes his head again, not saying a word. Whatever he says, he isn't telling us.

"We need to go up there." The words come from Manda. I turn and look at her in horror. What does she mean we need to go up there? Action required. But not by me.

"I agree," Bliss says, standing up. "We need to know what happened. Especially after what happened to Cook."

"What happened to Cook?" Manda asks. We quickly recap all that has happened in the past hour. Spying on Cohen, seeing the blood, seeing Cook's body. Even what Miss Loretta is going through.

"Bro, Camp NoTech can't close," Adam says, looking sad.

"None of that is going to matter now," Manda says to him. "Grab your bat and let's go. You guys take care of Andrei. Adam and I will check out what happened to Lin."

"No way," Cohen says. "I'm not letting you guys face that alone."

"Same here," says Bliss. Everyone looks at me.

"I'm with you guys," I answer. Not that there is a choice in the matter. Bliss leans back down and whispers something in Andrei's ear. Whatever it was seems to have a calming effect on him. He gets composed and stands up.

"Andrei is coming, too," he says. He stands, obviously still shaken. With that, we take off up the hill toward Cabin 9.

The rain will not relent, as if it is determined to drown us if we don't all end up dead. Again, I chuckle. Bliss shoots me a look. Which only makes me more uncomfortable and chuckle more.

"Lin has been hiding a laptop all summer," Andrei says. We are all walking slowly despite the downpour. I am thankful for the slow pace. I'd rather be soaking wet than face another dead body. The experience with Cook earlier was one too many dead bodies for me today.

"She hides it in the floor, underneath a loose board. She goes into the closet after the campers are in bed or during the afternoon after her elective is done. She plays this game called Rapture. She is like number 2 in the world. She thinks she hid it from me all summer, but Andrei knows everything. Well, except your name, Norm."

"I went there looking for her. She was really ticked that I made her dress like a killer and scare you guys. Andrei felt bad. I needed to make it right. But...she was in the closet... and..." He trails off, which is fine since we've made it to the cabin.

Adam goes in first, wielding his bat. Manda follows, then Andrei, Bliss, I, and Cohen bring up the rear. Bliss reaches back and grabs my hand as we go in. Nothing is stirring in the cabin. We all head to the counselor's area in the back corner. When we get there, Adam hesitates.

"I don't know if I can open it, bro." I feel relieved when Cohen makes his way to the front of the group. We all step back as he goes to open the closet door. He swings the door open and stands still. He stays like that for a bit. He bends down and reaches in, but thinks better about it.

"I don't think I should mess with this one. I have already tampered with one crime scene tonight." He gets up, crosses himself, and moves away. He leaves the door open. None of us moves. Andrei starts crying again. Even amazing myself, I move forward away from the rest of the group. Something inside needs to see this to understand what is happening. The rest move with me. I am never the leader. It feels unreal.

I see Lin lying in a heap. Her head had been beaten, and the weapon of choice is laying right by her. Blood covers most of the floor and the laptop. She looks like she could be sleeping. Poor Lin. She is so smart. Was smart. Manda makes a choking sound, holds her hand to her mouth, and makes a beeline for the bathroom. The rest of stay where we are. Bliss joins Andrei in the crying.

We hear a scream come from the bathroom.

Adam and his bat are off in a flash. We all follow him into the room. We find Manda on the floor opposite the last stall. She is backed under the sink and against the wall. She is screaming and pointing across from her. Adam reaches the end and is ready to swing away in the stall, but whatever is in there stops him in his tracks. Adam drops the bat and collapses with it. I am the next one there.

I wish I weren't.

I turn and stop Bliss. I fight to block her and Andrei from looking. But it is no good. They all see BB's body in the stall, head still missing. Andrei lets out another scream. Bliss starts crying. Cohen makes his way to the stall. He takes a long look. I don't know how long we have been standing there. It could have been a minute or hours. No one seems to know what to do. Finally, Cohen goes and helps Manda up. I move behind him to help Adam.

"Norm," he says, looking up at me with tears streaming down his face. "Norm, what is going on?" My heart breaks to see Adam like this. He is usually so vibrant. "It's BB, bro..." he chokes up as the words come out. I help him up and guide him away from the body. He is shivering in my arms. The rain is still bombarding the roof of the cabin. I start to get angry with it. Can't it stop raining this one time?

We make our way back to the main room. Cohen closes the closet door. Andrei has his arm around Manda. Bliss has her arm around Andrei. I have my arms around Adam, but I feel useless. Who can ever be prepared for something like this?

"Listen, guys," Cohen says, addressing us. "We need to get out of here now. Everyone, grab anything you need and meet me back at the main house. I will get your phones from the office. NO ONE goes anywhere by themselves. Andrei, you're with me. Norm, you're with Bliss. Manda and Adam. Can you guys handle it? They both nod without saying a word.

Everyone in agreement, we break apart. I am so thankful right now for Cohen to take charge. If he weren't here, I don't know who would step up. Who would be the voice of reason? Andrei is still crying. Manda is shaking. Adam is the quietest I've ever seen him. Bliss is in a daze, and I feel useless. This is a nightmare. Three dead bodies.

"We need someone to go and get Davis and Belle," Bliss adds. "Demarcus, too."

"We will," Cohen says. "Andrei and I will go get my keys and phone. Grab Andrei's stuff and grab the others. You with me, Andrei?" Bliss lets go of Andrei, and he nods.

"Ok, everyone, meet back at the main house in ten minutes. Don't separate, and yell like crazy if something happens." Cohen stares at us. He nods at us, grabs Andrei, and leaves.

Bliss and I watch as Manda and Adam head to their cabins, and Andrei runs next door to Cabin 8. He comes back out and heads to Cohen's cabin. I have a bad feeling about splitting like this, but I don't voice it.

"Let's get your stuff first," Bliss says.

CHAPTER EIGHTEEN

Cohen stops before entering his cabin. It is not because he is soaked by the rain. He is soaked, but the hesitation is for Andrei. He turns and faces the young man. Andrei is a mess. The 21-year-old is soaking wet. There are no traces of eyeliner and makeup anymore. His hair is wet and flat. They stopped by Andrei's cabin so he could grab some clothes and personal belongings. No makeup, though. No time for that now.

"Andrei, you OK with what you are about to see?" Andrei heard all about what happened to Cook and how Cohen brought the body here. But seeing it is a whole different thing. Andrei has already seen two dead bodies tonight. Cohen is having serious doubts about whether he can handle one more.

"I'm fine, Cohen. Andrei can handle this," he says with as much strength as he can.

They enter the cabin and find it exactly like Cohen had

left it. The blood trail leading from the front door to the kitchen has now dried. Cohen heads into his room to change out of the bloody overalls. He grabs his keys, his phone, and a gun that is hidden. He checks to make sure the clip is in and loaded. He never thought he would have to use this here. He takes one more look around and decides there is nothing else he can take or do right now. Time is tight.

When he returns to the living room, Andrei is gone. A quick search finds him in the kitchen, kneeling by Cook's body. Cohen kneels beside him and places his hand on Andrei's shoulder. To his credit, Andrei is holding it together better this time. There are still tears, but they are soft.

"I got what I need," Cohen whispers. "We need to get to the Main House." But Andrei doesn't move. He stays on his knees, looking at Cook. Cohen stands up, hoping Andrei will get the hint. When it is clear that he won't budge, Cohen settles down beside him again. The two sit in silence for a few seconds.

"This is all my fault," Andrei whispers.

"Andrei, you didn't kill Cook. I don't know who did, but I know it wasn't you."

"Not Cook, Cohen. It's Andrei's fault that Lin is dead." Andrei starts to cry harder now. "If I hadn't talked her into that stupid prank, she never would have gotten mad and gone back to her cabin. We should still be singing karaoke." Cohen pats Andrei's back. He lets him cry a little longer.

"Listen, Andrei. I am sorry for what happened to Lin, but sitting here now and talking about it isn't going to help us get out of here. Do you think she would want you to stick around Camp much longer?"

Andrei gets up from where Cook lies. Cohen hands him his clothes, and he goes to change. Cohen laughs a little as this is the first time all summer that Andrei has been shy about taking off his clothes in front of someone. Cohen takes one last look at Cook and turns off the lights. Andrei reenters the room. A change of clothes makes him look fresh, a new person.

"We need to go check on Demarcus and the others," Cohen says.

"Andrei is ready."

They make their way back outside. The rain has let up, but the wind is still strong. They make their way back downhill. They check all three cabins for Demarcus, Davis, and Belle, but find no one. They are thankful that they also find no blood or bodies. It is when they come out of Belle's cabin that they hear a scream.

"It sounds like it is coming from Bliss's cabin," Cohen says. He looks at his watch and pauses. He is conflicted on what to do.

"Andrei, listen to me." Cohen starts to take his keys out. "I need you to get to the Main House. Someone has to call the police." He moves through the keys on the ring and shows him a big gold one. "This is the key to get into Miss Loretta's office. Use the phone and call 911."

"What about not splitting up? Andrei needs to stick with you."

"We don't have time for that. I need to see what is going on at Bliss' cabin, and I need you to be strong. Here. Take this." Cohen pulls out the gun. Andrei's eyes widen, and he shakes his head.

"No, no, no, no, no. Andrei doesn't do guns."

"Take it, Andrei." Cohen shoves it into Andrei's hands. "You don't have to shoot anyone if you don't want to. If something happens, you run away and hide somewhere safe. Fire the gun into the air, and I will find you. But Andrei, you need to do this. And now."

Andrei holds the gun and stares at it, then back at Cohen. Cohen nods his head, seeming to reassure Andrei one more time. He looks toward Bliss' cabin and takes off. Andrei watches him go.

When Cohen is a few feet away, Andrei tucks the gun in his jeans and heads to the Main House. The whole walk, he is shaking with fear. He never thought of Camp NoTech as a scary place. But as he is walking along the path, he jumps at every slight noise. Finally, he gives up and starts to run. The sooner he gets there, the sooner he can call.

He makes his way through the back door and into the kitchen. He can't believe that it has only been a few hours since he was in here with a busted nose. It seems like a lifetime ago. He enters the living room, still lit up from the party. Everything is clean and back to normal. Andrei notices the axe and machete against the wall and goes to pick up the axe. He rushes over to Miss Loretta's office to unlock the door.

But it is already unlocked.

The door has been busted open at the lock. Andrei uses the axe to push the door open. Miss Loretta's office is dark with only the light from the living room shining in. Her office chair is turned the other way, and someone is sitting in it.

"Demarcus, is that you?"

Andrei waits for the answer that never comes. He enters the office, flicks the lights on, and moves around the chairs toward Miss Loretta's desk. He works his way around the desk, pushes the chair around.

Andrei lets out a blood-chilling scream.

Seated in the office chair is Demarcus, at least what is left of Demarcus. He has two knives sticking in his head and a giant hole in his chest where Big Daddy went through. His eyes are still open, showing the shock of what happened. Andrei's eyes look very similar. He backs up against the window in shock. He forgets about the axe in his hand, dropping it to the floor.

Just then, the lights go out.

Another scream escapes.

Andrei reaches down and picks up the axe. He makes his way back into the living room slowly. As he enters the dark room, he remembers what Cohen said.

"OK, Andrei. You need to run somewhere safe," he tells himself. Just then, the lights come back on.

Andrei is not alone.

The door shuts behind him, and Andrei turns around. Before he can even register the man with the gas mask is there, the machete that was left out comes swinging down, hitting him on the side of the head, into his right eye. Andrei falls on his knees, and another swipe comes down. Andrei falls to his side and rolls over onto his back. The man takes swipe after swipe at Andrei. The blood splatters onto his checkered jacket and mask as he chops away.

CHAPTER NINETEEN

B liss and I stop at my cabin, and I run in to grab some clothes. I also take my keys and wallet. If we need to make an escape, I want to be ready to go fast. I step into my bathroom and change out of my wet clothes. We head back to the door. I stop and take one final look around Cabin 2. I was supposed to be in Cabin 1, but then Adam informed me that "Adam Bombs are number 1." So, Cabin 2 became my home.

I remember walking on the first day. Standing just inside the door, I admired what I saw. I had been to many camps as a child—theater, church, Boy Scouts—but nothing was even close to this nice. The smell of the wood mixed with cleaning detergents welcomed me. Of course, after ten weeks of stinky boys, the smell was quite different. I still had chairs in a circle in the middle of the room. Eleven chairs, one for each camper and one for myself. This is where they had family time each night before bed. I always made sure that my campers knew I cared about them. I wasn't Adam or Davis, who would just ignore them as soon as dinner was done. It was this closeness that I attribute to the large bonuses I received from parents this summer.

This was not how I thought the final night of camp would go. I figured I would tolerate the party as long as I could before everyone got wasted. Then I would walk Bliss back to her cabin and hit the sack. From what I was told, clean-up and repair day is the hardest day of the year. You work all day, on top of being sad that it was the end of the summer. No way did I think that the night would go from kissing Manda, finding Cook's body in Cohen's cabin, to Lin and BB, and now standing here readying to leave. Not the way I thought this night would go at all.

"We need to get going," Bliss says, interrupting my thoughts. She links her arm in mine for one last look.

"Just thinking about the summer and the first time I came in here."

"I know." She rests her head on my arm. I let out a big sigh.

"Let's get your stuff and meet up with the others."

We make our way up to Bliss' cabin, but I stop her from going in.

"I should go in first," I say, moving her behind me.

"You really are taking this 'girls want to be safe' thing to heart, aren't you?" I smile back at her.

"Sure am. Plus, I am bigger and can block you if someone is in there." I open the screen door, turn the knob, and go in.

No one attacks me.

I flip the lights on, and the cabin looks normal. The beds are all messed up from the last day, trunks left open. That smell of perfume and hair product still lingers in the air. It stings my eyes.

I let Bliss come in, and she heads to her space. I see her dig into a drawer and pull out some sketch pads. Before I know it, she is stripping off her clothes. I look away, giving her some privacy. I look out the window and notice the rain has died down again. I hope that is the end of the storm.

BANG!

I startle at the noise. I turn, and Bliss is looking at the back of the cabin where the bathrooms are. I put my finger up to my mouth, telling her to stay quiet. I wave her over to me. We are now standing in the center of the cabin, waiting to hear if there will be another bang and where it is coming from.

BANG!

This time it comes from the side of the cabin.

"We need a weapon," I hear Bliss whisper to me. I start to look around, not really seeing anything of much use. Before I can grab her, Bliss runs over to her dresser and opens a drawer. After searching for a while, she comes back carrying something silver in her hands. It is a knife. A switchblade, to be exact. I give her a quizzical look.

"This is my father's. He always insisted I keep one. I never thought I would have any need for it." She unfolds it, and a 6-inch blade comes out. It wasn't much. I reach out and take it from her.

"Let me have it," I say. Action is required.

BANG!

We turn to face the front door where the sound was this time. I wait, half expecting someone to bust down the door and ambush us. But nothing happens. We both turn to the other side of the cabin. The one that we haven't heard a sound from.

BANG!

The sound comes a few seconds later.

"If they are going around the cabin, I bet they will go to the back again," I say to Bliss. A plan starts to form in my head. I move Bliss over to her space and open the closet door. "Wait here. I'm going out there."

"No, you're not," she says. "We are supposed to stick together."

"I am going to go outside and start shouting. Whoever is out there will come after me. I will run away, and you can escape. Head to the Main House and meet up with everyone else."

"This is not a good idea."

"You are mine to keep safe, remember?" I push into the closet, and she hugs me before I shut the door. I still have her knife as I make my way across the room to the front door. I pause.

BANG!

Right on cue, the sounds come full circle to the back of the cabin. I step out and yell.

"HEY! HEY! I'm over here! Come get me!" I scream as loudly as I can and run to the side of the cabin. No one is there. I scream again, trying to draw the person out. I run to the back. No one is there. That is when I hear it.

A scream coming from inside the cabin.

I run up the steps to the back door. It won't budge. I bang my shoulder against it, but nothing happens. I pound on it, screaming for Bliss. Why did I leave her there alone? I take off around the other side and go for the front door. It, too, won't budge. Another scream comes from inside the cabin. I pound on the door.

"COME OUT HERE! LEAVE HER ALONE." I pick up the chair sitting in front of the cabin and bang it against the door. It does nothing but shatter apart, falling to the ground. Over and over, I bang my body against the door. It won't move.

That is when I hear a giant *WHOOSH!*

I look in the window next to the front door and see flames everywhere. A large man wearing a gas mask is dragging Bliss across the floor. She is screaming and fighting.

Who is this man? Is this Able Dunn? This is not Andrei in a mask. I can tell by the way he lifts Bliss off the floor. I look down at the ground, searching for anything that will help. I see a large rock, so I drop the knife and pick up the rock. I step and throw it through the window, shattering the glass. The heat escapes the cabin, making it so hot that I'm forced to move away. Away from Bliss, I need to be going toward here. If action is ever required, it is now!

"Bliss! Bliss!" I scream.

I watch as the man holds Bliss in front of him, takes a knife, and slits her throat from ear to ear. Blood gushes out and covers the front of the dry clothes she just put on.

I scream again.

This can't be happening. I have to save her. I move toward the window, but the heat is getting stronger. It makes me step back again. The man leaves, letting Bliss fall to her knees. She puts her hands up, trying to stop the bleeding, but it is useless.

I look into her eyes as life leaves them. I know what her face is saying; you were supposed to keep me safe.

CHAPTER TWENTY

Time: 5:04 A.M.
Place: One Road In, One Road Out

Miss Loretta is exhausted as she makes her way back to camp. She spent the whole Friday night into Saturday morning working hard. Going into Rock Creek and spending her night schmoozing rich people in order to save the camp is not her way of enjoying herself. It is, however, the only reason she keeps her membership to the Rock Creek Country Club. RCCC is the best place in town to get some of the more wealthy people to part ways with their hard-earned cash. So, it means tight pants and skirts, low-cut tops, and flirting with them all. The women, too. At least she hadn't stooped as low as trying to actually trade sex for money. But the flirting she could handle. Tonight it paid off.

She has just deposited a check for $10,000 given to her by the illustrious Rhonda Black. Miss Black had discovered way too late in life, and after two failed marriages with no kids, that she preferred to make some good happen in this world. After a few months of working together, Rhonda Black invested in the camp. It was at least enough to pay the rest of the bills and give her a head start on next year's camp. She would have nine whole months to continue to fundraise, but $10,000 is a HUGE head start. It is also enough excitement to keep her awake on the way home. Rock Creek is only five minutes to Camp NoTech, but it's a grueling 20-minute drive in and out of camp. Straight downhill one way, and straight uphill the other way.

Not for the first time, she is thankful for Cohen and his work there. She is looking forward to sleeping as long as she can before she has to get up and say goodbye to her counselors. What a great group she had this year. Most have expressed interest in coming next year, but she will have to wait and see what happens after she lets them know that their pay will be decreased next year. Hopefully, the fact that many of the families give bonuses will encourage them to come back. She will have to do less advertising this year, as well. That $10,000 has to stretch far.

She makes the big, steep turn that makes her final descent into the valley where Camp NoTech rests. She gets a full view of the camp. The Main House lights are still on. No surprise there. The kids are probably still partying or passed out. Most of the lights are off in the cabins. She smiles at her lampposts that adorn the walkway. She is going to put them on a timer next year. After the 10 p.m. lights out, they will stay on for another hour, and that should save some money. She figured the cabins that move down the lake are also lights out.

She hits the big dip at the end of the hill and levels off. She is passing under the Camp NoTech sign. It, too, stays lit up all night. Why? She didn't really know. She makes a mental note to have it turned off at night next summer. Just burning money.

She grips the wheel slightly as she makes the last turn into the camp. She isn't expecting anything, so when a large figure steps in front of her, she swerves at the last moment. Her shiny silver truck comes to rest by hitting a pole across from the Main House. Miss Loretta bangs her head against the steering wheel, cutting open a small gash. She is dazed, and it takes her a few moments to come to. When she does, she is confused by what she saw. Did a person really jump in front of her? Or was she feeling the effects of a late night and the alcohol?

She feels the blood running down her face and grabs some paper towels from the glove compartment. She presses them against her head and tries to get the bleeding to stop. She stays like that for a minute, trying to recover and straighten out exactly what happened. Her truck is smoking from the hood, and it looks like there is some damage. This does not help her recovery. She crawls out of the truck. She feels woozy when she finally stands up straight. She looks down at her top. It is ruined by the blood, which still hasn't stopped. She presses down hard on her forehead and heads up the steps.

The first thing she notices when she enters is Andrei's body.

Miss Loretta doesn't seem to process what she is seeing. Is there really a body on the floor? Is that Andrei? Is he dead? What is going on? Blood is splattered everywhere and all over the floor. She moves back toward the door and closes her eyes. When she feels the spinning stop, she opens them again. The scene is the same. That is when it hits her. Something very bad has happened here. She looks around to see if there is anyone or anything else around. When she sees nothing, she moves toward her office. She steps over an axe lying by Andrei. She sees a gun poking out of Andrei's pants. She thinks about picking it up right now; she only has one free hand.

She doesn't stop to answer why her office door is open or why it's busted at the lock. She just hurries in to get the phone.

Then, she sees Demarcus.

This time, Miss Loretta doesn't stop to tell if this is real life or not. She bends over and empties the contents of her stomach on her office floor. The sight of the puke and blood from her head almost makes her pass out. It takes a few seconds, but she finally stands again. She reaches for the phone, picks it up, and holds it to her ear.

There is a dial tone.

Miss Loretta says a small prayer and dials 911.

"911, what is your emergency?" the female operator says.

"Yes. This is Loretta Parks at Camp NoTech in the valley. There are two dead bodies here."

"Ok, stay with me. Two dead bodies, you say?"

"Yes," Miss Loretta says, and she starts crying.

"Stay with me, ma'am. We have an officer en route now."

"Thank you. I am in the Main House. The bodies are there..."

Then, the phone goes dead.

"Hello? Hello?" Miss Loretta screams into the phone. She holds the phone to her ear, but there is nothing but silence on the other end. That is when she hears a noise from the front room. She drops the phone and hides underneath her desk. Her body is getting covered as she squeezes as tight as she can under the desk. Demarcus' body is right by her, and she is tempted to puke again. Her breathing is hard, and she has to force herself to be quiet when she hears the office door swing open. Heavy boots walk across the floor.

They stop. Miss Loretta waits for what feels like an eternity. No movement. "Maybe they are gone," she thinks. The shivers of her body are so violent that she is amazed they aren't shaking the entire desk. Finally, the heavy boots start to move away. She lets out a short breath, hoping the footsteps will continue out into the living room.

They don't.

In a swift move, the boots move across the floor, and the desk is flipped over. Standing above is the man she saw who jumped in front of her. She gasps as she notices the gas mask. It can't be! Before she can register anything, an axe swings down, stabbing into her chest. Again, another strike. Then, another and another. The final blow comes, and the axe is left in her.

Miss Loretta is dead.

CHAPTER TWENTY-ONE

I fall to my knees, and tears fill my eyes. The cabin continues to burn in front of me, and I am tempted to walk straight into it. She is dead. Bliss is dead.

I didn't keep her safe.

I don't fight back the tears. I should have tried harder. I should never have left her alone. I was trying for once in my life to take the action required! Why did I try to be the hero? Play it safe... I always played it safe. Why didn't I play it safe now! The fire is really starting to engulf the cabin now. The heat that is coming toward me now is almost unbearable. I don't move. I deserve it.

I don't know how long I'm in the heat, but soon I find myself being pulled away.

"No! NO!" I cry out. I deserve to burn. I deserve to die with Bliss.

"Norm! NORM!" I hear someone calling my name, but I don't respond. All I can keep seeing is Bliss' face as she dropped to her knees. The image of blood flowing from her throat all over her front is indescribable. I feel nothing but sickness and pain. Death in the fire would be a welcomed relief compared to seeing that image in my mind for the rest of my life. I struggle against whoever is pulling me back.

I didn't keep her safe. The sentence repeats itself over and over in my head.

"Leave me alone!" I scream.

"Norm. Look at me." I am dragged farther away from the cabin. Eventually, I run out of steam and stop resisting. I vaguely look up and see Cohen's face coming into focus. Why is he here? Where are the others? I bury my head into him and cry. Bliss is gone, and it's my fault.

My mind starts rolling like an old film reel. I see flashes of her from the summer. The first day, when she walked in. The first time she read her poetry to me. The time I was sick, she brought me soup from Demarcus. I think about the time she drew caricatures of all of us. The day Miss Loretta had a meltdown, she took charge of the whole camp. She is amazing. We were going to do big things.

I didn't keep her safe.

"We have to get out of here." Cohen is practically dragging me away. I have no desire to leave, no desire to be. Life means nothing. I found someone who accepted me, made me feel special, who I could talk to about anything, and she is gone. I don't move. I won't move. Whoever that man was in the gas mask can come for me next. I will sit here and make it easy for him.

"What is going on?" I hear more footsteps running toward us. I glance to see Adam and Manda make their way to us. Manda takes one look at me, one look at the cabin, one look at Cohen, and then back at me. She puts the pieces together.

"No! NO! NO! NO!" she says, tears starting to rise. Adam looks at Manda, at me, at Cohen, back to Manda. He doesn't put it together.

"Adam, help me here," Cohen says, starting to lift me. It takes both of them to get me to my feet. Manda keeps asking me what happened, but I don't say anything. I ignore her. Somehow, they get me moving away from the cabin. I don't look back. I don't need to. I can still see Bliss. The blood.

I didn't keep her safe.

We finally made our way to the gazebo, where I collapsed on a bench. I try to shut everything out. The sound of the fire, the smell of the smoke, and the others talking to me. I just want to escape. The tears finally stop; I don't think I have any left in me. I want to go away.

"James," Manda says. I can tell she is kneeling next to me. She places her hand on my arm. A few hours ago, that would have been the highlight of my night. Now it just racks me with guilt. I don't deserve the gesture.

"James," she says again. "What happened?" I say nothing. I continue to lie on the bench, facing away from her.

"Bro." Adam is there now, too. "Hey, Bro. Come on. What happened up there?"

"Leave him alone, guys," I hear Cohen say.

"No," I hear Manda say. "Where is Bliss? What happened in the cabin? It's ON FIRE!" I hear her crouch back down and put her hand on my back. "James, listen to me. I know something bad happened, but you need to talk to me." I hear her start to cry, and I feel like I am about to vomit. "Please, James. What happened?"

I don't want to relive it. I don't want to say it. But I do.

I roll around and managed to relay to them what happened. The noises outside, leaving her alone, the doors being blocked, and, finally, the fire. There is stunned silence. Everyone is staring at me. They know what I did.

"I didn't keep her safe," I whisper.

"No, bro!" Adam grabs me by the shoulders and looks me

dead in the eyes. "Listen, bro. That is not true. Not at all. You went outside, bro. You went out to sacrifice yourself for her. You were brave. You can't sit here and think otherwise. Listen. You did keep her safe." Adam's eyes are so fierce and focused on me that I actually believe what he is saying. A little.

"James," Manda says. "She knew that. She knew you were there and trying to save her. This is not your fault. Do you hear me?" Cohen, too, bends down to where they are all three in front of me.

"Nor...I mean, James, this is terrible. I know this is awful for you three, for all of us. But listen, we have to keep moving," Cohen says. "This guy, whoever he is, is still out here. You three have to get to the Main House and get out of here." I hear what he is saying. I want to do what he is saying. I just don't want anyone else hurt. I nod my head.

"What do you mean, us three?" Manda asks. We all stand up and face Cohen.

"Yeah, bro. We are not splitting up." Adam challenges. But Cohen looks at us with seriousness in his eyes. I know I am not going to like what he is about to say.

"I am going to look for the others. We need to find the others and get them to safety, too. I sent Andrei up there to call the authorities. Get there, get Andrei, get a car, and leave. We will be right behind you. Don't worry. Now, go!" He doesn't give us a chance to respond. He takes off out of the gazebo and leaves us standing there. We all holler at him, but he ignores our pleas. Adam starts to head out after him, but I grab him.

"He is right," I say. "We need to get out of here. I don't want to be here anymore."

"Who do you think was in the cabin?" Manda asks.

"I think it was Able Dunn."

"That can't be possible," Adam says in shock.

"Whoever it was, he isn't going to stop. There was no remorse. No shame. No guilt. It was cold and heartless." I look at them both. I see the information start to sink into their brains. Manda heaves her shoulders and takes charge.

"Let's get to the Main House and get the hell out of here."

CHAPTER TWENTY-TWO

W e take off and make our way up the steps to the Main House. No one speaks, and as luck would have it, the rain starts up again. I am normally one who is all for rain. I love it. Tonight would have been a great night to sleep with the cabin windows open and enjoy the sound. Sleep is not something I have even thought about. I start to make my way to the back of the house.

"If we are going to go in the back door, then we need to be ready for anything. There is no telling if he is in there or if there is more than one of them. Whatever is about to happen, we need to be ready." Manda says to us.

"I'll go first." Adam steps ahead of us. He raises the baseball bat and looks prepared to hit a home run at anyone who is in there. We place Manda between us, and we go up the stairs. Adam swings open the door.

I am expecting the worst. But if there was a psycho maniac killer waiting in the kitchen of the Main House to kill us, he isn't there right now. Adam stops us at the top of the stairs while he goes in to inspect the kitchen and look in the pantry. He comes back and waves us in. The last time I was in here, Demarcus was fixing us dinner. At that moment, the kitchen smelled of spices, herbs, and glorious smells. Now it is cold, dark, and lifeless. Sterile. It is a wonderful contrast to our lives right now. Adam searches all the drawers and comes up with a large flashlight, a knife, and a hammer. He gives Manda the knife and gives me the hammer. We all look at each other as if to say, "What else is the rest of this night going to bring?"

We assemble in our order again. Adam first, then Manda, and me in the rear. The flashlight casts a large beam ahead of us into the living room, making it easy to see what is awaiting us.

Andrei.

Manda screams and drops her knife. She buries her head in my chest. I wrapped my arms around her and shut my eyes. Too late. The image of Andrei's mangled body is burned forever.

Lying on his back, his neck and shoulder areas are a mess. The bloody machete is next to him, and I can visualize the man whacking him over and over again. It makes me sick. Who is this guy? Adam walks over to Andrei's body and kneels to shut Andrei's eyes. Manda turns around, and we both watch the ceremonial gesture.

"We need to call the cops," Adam says and heads into Miss Loretta's office, walking slowly, ready to swing. Manda and I stay in the main room. I can't believe that Andrei is like this. Such a vibrant, eccentric person now lies like this.

A giant scream escapes from the office.

Manda and I rush in, and we see Adam standing over Miss Loretta's body, which has an axe still sticking out of it.

"Brooooooooooo! NO!" Adam is screaming.

Manda lets out another scream. We look up to see her pointing at Demarcus's body sitting in the chair. I back up into the door, closing it. I can't believe what I am seeing.

Andrei, Miss Loretta, Demarcus—all dead. Adding in everything else from this night, I am close to giving up again. Overwhelming is an understatement. And the smell! Both bodies are making the room stink of blood and flesh. If the sight doesn't make you sick, the smell will.

Adam can't take it anymore and starts destroying everything in the room with the bat. He is raving mad, hitting bookshelves, lamps, anything he can find. Manda is trying to get him to call down, but he won't. He is about to smash everything on the floor when he stops mid-swing. He drops the bat and reaches down for something. It is the phone! t

"I'm going to call 911," Adam says. Manda moves back toward me, and we watch him raise the receiver to his ear. He listens and clicks the phone over and over. With another scream, he turns and smashes it against the wall.

"It's dead!"

My stomach drops. This is not good. Not good at all. The only line we have to the outside is cut off. We can't stay here a second longer. Where is Cohen? We need to go. Adam picks up the bat and starts heading across the office. He has to maneuver his way around the bodies and chaos. He reaches a large chest, flings it open, and brings out a box. It's our phones.

"That's it," I say. "I got my keys. Let's get out of here.'

"What about Cohen?" Manda asks. "He went to get Davis and Belle."

"Not waiting. We need to leave right now."

"I'm with you, bro."

Manda gives us both a look of total disgust.

"How can you guys say that? Are we really going to leave them here? Leave them so they can end up like this?" She points to the ground where Miss Loretta is.

I know she is right, but I can't shake this feeling that we need to leave right now. Hop in my truck and go. I feel like I should have more courage than I do. I should be yelling at them, forcing them to go. Or I should just leave them.

"She is right. No one else can end up like this." I know then it's settled. They aren't going to leave the others, and I won't leave them. We are stuck here, fighting whoever is out there. I hope that Cohen gets here quickly with the others so we can leave.

We head out of the office. Manda takes the axe from Miss Loretta's body. I look at my hammer and pick up the machete that was lying by Andrei. We lock both the back and front doors. We wait.

Manda finds some matches and goes around the room lighting some candles. Miss Loretta had this thing for giant candles that look like bowls. Of all of the places that I have ever sat and waited before, this room with a dead body is not my top pick. With the rain, the wind, lightning, thunder, the bodies, the tiredness, the candles, the fear, and the guilt, this is the worst place ever.

Then, it got worse.

We hear him before we can see him. A large bang comes from the kitchen, and we realize it's the sound of someone breaking through the back door. Glass breaking, wood breaking, we hear it all crash onto the kitchen floor. Before we can escape out the front, he is in the living room. We take off to the other side, back against the wall in the area where the karaoke was set up. A thought runs through my mind of what song I should sing right now. Maybe if we were entertaining enough, he would leave us alone. I let out a chuckle.

"Well, Norm is nervous," Adam says. The man is now standing just inside the doorway of the kitchen, where we enjoyed our meal earlier tonight. Irony. Standing right where Cohen told us all about Able Dunn stands Able Dunn. We are backed up as far as we can go. Adam with his bat. Manda with an axe. I hold a machete.

"We are not going down without a fight, bro." I don't know if Adam is talking to himself, to us, or Dunn. Able starts to make his way across the room, taking slow, deliberate steps. The rain is pounding, the wind is howling, the lightning is flashing, and the thunder is booming. He is about halfway there when he picks up the pace. We grip our weapons. We are ready for him.

We are about to attack when a gunshot rings out. It hits Dunn in the back, and he stops. I look past Dunn and see Cohen standing, holding a blood-covered gun, and it is aimed at Dunn. Dunn turns around and faces Cohen.

"Get out of here, guys," Cohen says to us.

"What about the others?" Manda asks. Cohen gets a pained look and shakes his head.

Dunn moves toward Cohen and rings out another shot, hitting him dead center. It stops Dunn, but he doesn't fall, he doesn't take a knee, nothing. Like a pebble hit him.

"GO! Get to where Cook is," Cohen yells at us. "I will be there in a minute." We take off toward the front door. Dunn shows us no worry. I unlock the front door, and we take off running toward Cohen's cabin. The rain has made the ground a wreck, and I slip and fall behind the others. I lie on the ground, looking up at the rain falling on me. I decide I am fine right here. I am exhausted, and the rain feels nice coming down on my face. I close my eyes and let the water soak me. This is a good place to die.

"Get up, bro!" Adam comes back and jerks me off the ground. He looks at me and I nod to say I'm ok, I'm there. We take off down the hill. As we approach, we hear gunshots ring out from the main house. I hope that Cohen is giving Able Dunn what he deserves. We run up the steps, through Cohen's front door, and slam it shut.

CHAPTER TWENTY-THREE

**Time: 5:49 A.M.
Location: The Main House**

The three counselors have escaped through the front
door, leaving Cohen face-to-face with Able Dunn.
The first bullets shot out of the gun that Cohen is
still holding had no effect on the monster. So, now it is a face-
off.

Dunn stands there motionless. His arms are at his side,
and his chest is heaving. Cohen never flinches. He holds the
gun steady, aimed and ready to fire again. From where he is
standing, he can see into the office. He sees Miss Loretta's
body on the floor and Demarcus still sitting in the chair.
Then, he knows it. Whatever he has to do, he will stop Able
Dunn tonight. He will not let the remaining counselors have
the same fate. Even if it means his life will end.

"This stop right here, Able." Dunn's head tilts. Is that an
acknowledgment of his name? Does he recognize his own
name anymore? How long has it been since he heard it, heard
any other human's voice in a conversational manner?

"It is Able, right? Able Dunn?" Cohen speaks in a soft voice, but still doesn't let the gun relax. "This used to be your land. All this was your father's and your grandfather's. Is that why you did what you did tonight? You figure it's time for revenge for your old man?"

Dunn still doesn't move.

"Or was it for mommy? Was that it, Able? You wanted to do all this for your dear mother?" There is a noticeable physical response to the mention of Dunn's mother. His breath quickens, his hands clench. No one can see behind the gas mask, but if you could, I am sure you would see an anger indescribable.

"Your mother?" Cohen continues. "Mommy is the reason for all this carnage tonight? Do you think that you can take the lives of all these people to justify the taking of your land? You gave up your land, Able." Cohen takes a small step forward, gun still raised and pointed.

"Why are you here now, Able? Why tonight? Why did you choose tonight? And where have you been? Have you been in that shelter? Waiting for the right moment to come back?" Able is barely holding it together now. You can hear grunts and growls coming from under the mask, an animal sound. The sound of someone who hasn't spoken in years.

"Do you want to say something, Able? Do you want to explain yourself to me? Tell me your secrets. Tell me what Daddy used to do to you? To the other people who came here?" Cohen's voice grows louder and more sinister with each question. His muscles grip the gun.

Like a frenzied animal, Dunn charges. Cohen fires the gun, hitting him in the chest. It doesn't stop him. Another shot and another shot, hitting again in the front. Dunn stumbles a bit and stops moving. A hand raises to touch the blood that is coming out.

But he doesn't stop.

The final two shots shoot out, finally dropping Dunn to his knees. Both hands are on his chest, covered in blood. A gurgling noise sounds out from under that mask.

Able Dunn drops face-first to the floor.

Cohen stands there, smelling the gunpowder in the air. He waits. Dunn doesn't move. Cohen can see the blood pooling out from underneath the body. Cohen waits a minute longer before he moves.

He makes his way over to the body of Able Dunn. Taking his time, he uses his foot to kick the carcass. The first time was very soft, but then harder and harder. Then, no movement. Able Dunn does nothing but lie there with his blood pouring out. Only then does Cohen drop the gun.

He moves to the office to take a look at the bodies in there. He sees the phone lying on the floor, picks it up, and finds the same result. He kneels by Miss Loretta's body.

"Oh, Loretta. What has happened?' He closes her eyelids and heads back out of the office.

Able Dunn is no longer on the floor.

Dunn grabs Cohen by the neck and lifts him. He turns and tosses Cohen across the room. Cohen is dazed. He tries to stand, but Dunn races across the room. He picks Cohen up again and slams his head through the glass of a front window. He lies there in the broken glass, blood starting to come out.

Dunn grabs him again, moves a few feet down, and busts his head through another window. The blood now openly flows out of Cohen's face. He is picked up and tossed across the room. He hits the wall hard and falls to the floor. He lies there bleeding. He is finally able to push himself up and sit with his back to the wall. Through the blood, he sees Dunn staring at him.

"What are you waiting for, Able?" Cohen taunts. Able reaches down and picks up the hammer that was left earlier.

He looks at it and then goes back to Cohen. Cohen, whose face is completely covered in blood, just laughs.

"Do what you must, Able."

Dunn charges forward. Cohen doesn't resist as Dunn takes the hammer and starts beating Cohen on the head. Such force is coming down upon him that the hammer drives deeper and deeper into Cohen's head. A large dent forms in the space where his forehead and right eye should be. Down and down again, the hammer comes, well past what is needed to finish off Cohen. Dunn is possessed. Even when the head is half beaten in and it is nothing but sloppy wet goo, he still drives the hammer down. Grunt and grunt go along with the hammer.

When he stops, Cohen's head is barely recognizable. Pieces of hair and an eye are all that is left.

CHAPTER TWENTY-FOUR

Time: 6:01 A.M.
Location: One Road In, One Road Out

Officer Glen Spencer is sipping his morning coffee and taking his time making the long trek down into the valley. Spencer had just come on duty at the Rock Creek Police Department when the call from the camp came in. Being a 10-year veteran of the RCPD, he doesn't know why he still volunteers for these early morning weekend shifts. He groans, and he realizes he'd rather be here than at home with his overbearing wife. He'd rather be sipping bad coffee and driving 15 miles an hour than listen to her bug him all Saturday about the lawn, about the gutters, about finances. Yes, he would much rather be here.

The call that came in was hard to hear and a garbled mess, but they could make out Miss Loretta saying something. With nothing else to do, Spencer volunteered to make the drive out. If anything, the camp has great coffee and food, so maybe he would get lucky and get a nice meal out of the trip. He always loves going by throughout the week for a routine checkup at the camp. Miss Loretta was very nice to look at, and the food is good.

With the windows down, Spencer is enjoying the drive. It is still dark, no light, pre-dawn, and the air is cool. As soon as you go a mile down in the valley, you start to lose radio signal. Every once in a while, you will get a blast of sound and can hear the dispatch, but this morning it was ruining Spencer's vibe, so he just clicked it off. He settles down and takes another sip of coffee.

Word was that Miss Loretta wasn't into dating anymore, but that didn't stop Spencer from fantasizing during his drive down. He does this often when he is not home. In some alternate world of his, he would show up this morning and knock on Miss Loretta's door. She would open it up, greet him with a kiss, wondering why he was there. Then, she would reward him for his service by inviting him in. Now that would be even better than good coffee and a meal.

He makes the final turn that leads into camp. As the camp comes into view, he can see lights flickering in the distance. Is that a fire? He can't tell from here, but it makes him pick up his speed. He can't go too fast because he really doesn't want to wreck the cruiser and spend all day dealing with that. But he does speed up as fast as he dares.

He starts to get nervous now as he drives closer to the camp. The smooth, relaxed vibe of a few moments ago is long gone. He can smell the smoke now in the air, and he is getting worried. He enters under the lit-up Camp NoTech sign and heads toward the main house, where the lights are still burning. If someone is up at this hour, then something must be happening. He parks by Miss Loretta's crashed truck and hops out. He looks into the truck cab and can see the blood on her face.

He hustles back to the cruisers and turns the radio on. Nothing.

"This is Officer Spencer requesting assistance at Camp NoTech. Over." He waits and hopes for a reply, but hears nothing. He repeats the command, but with the same results. He sits there, pondering what to do next. He checks his sidearm to make sure it's ready, and he steps back out of the car. He makes his way toward the house. He steps partway up the stairs when he sees the busted windows and blood. He pulls his gun out and makes his way through the front door.

Officer Spencer pukes.

The sight of Andrei and Cohen makes him double over. Once he is done emptying the contents of his stomach, he stands up and regroups. Pale-faced and sweating, he raises his gun and makes his way toward the office. He has been here enough times to know his way around. He goes past the dead bodies but tries to avoid looking at them.

What he sees in the office is worse.

Spencer is stunned and can't move as he takes in the sight of the two bodies. Seeing Miss Loretta mutilated was not the sight he was expecting to see. He moves back out of the office, past the other two bodies, and back out the door. He runs back to his cruiser. He climbs into the front seat and grabs the radio. He screams for backup, calling for all rein-forcements, but there is still no sound. He clicks it off and on again to see if that will help reboot the signal. Still nothing.

He continues to scream into the radio, asking for help. He finally throws the radio down in anger. What is he going to do? Trying to calm himself down, he finally hears the cackle of the radio coming to life. He lets out a yelp and digs down onto the cruiser floor, trying to locate it. He has to throw coffee cups and fast food wrappers all around. He finally finds it and sits back up.

"Thank you, God. Thank you, God. Thank you, God," he mutters as he fumbles with the receiver, trying to get it to face the right way. He clicks on it and is about to speak with a hand reaches through the open window, yanking him out of the car. Spencer no longer has hold of the radio or his gun that rests on the floor amongst the cups and wrappers.

Dunn picks up the officer and busts his head through the back window of the car. He pulls him back out and drops down to one knee. He takes Spencer's head and puts it between the door and the car. He starts to slam the cruiser door. Dunn's arm muscles tense and bulge as he squeezes and slams it over and over, ending the life of Officer Glen Spencer. Once the sides of the head are caved in, Dunn throws the body on the ground and stands up. He looks around, trying to get a sense of direction. The skies erupt again with a massive downpour. He gets a bearing on the location and takes off.

He is headed straight for Cohen's cabin.

CHAPTER TWENTY-FIVE

Adam and Manda have the same reaction to Cook's body that I did. Stunned, appalled, sad. Cohen's kitchen is white. White floors, white cabinets, white appliances. It would seem that someone decided that an insane asylum was the look to go for here. With all the white, it makes the bloody sheet surrounding Cook's body stand out even more.

We all sit and wait. Manda leans her head on Adam's shoulder, and I sit across the room from them. We all take the time to relax and try to recoup some energy. I have not run that much since high school, when we were forced to run a mile every year. At the beginning of school each year, someone had the bright idea that every single student in the United States had to run a mile in under 10 minutes. If that student was unable to do so in the first attempt, then the student must run it over and over again until the 10-minute mark is broken. Therefore, I averaged three to four times a year. I can't explain the embarrassment I felt each year as everyone was done with the mile and enjoying fun games, while I was still out there running. Now I would happily run 20 miles to erase tonight. Bliss's face appears in my mind.

I didn't keep her safe.

Maybe the person who thought up the yearly 10-minute mile had once been in a situation where people were getting killed on the last night of camp. Perhaps it was the catalyst for this program. They figured if you could run a mile in 10 minutes, you could survive running for your life around a campground. If the program was for the benefit of us being chased by psycho killers, then the mile should be run in the middle of the night, with pouring rain, with a maniac chasing you.

I rest my head against the wall and close my eyes. I am tempted to let the exhaustion have its way. I don't even know what to think anymore. This night has been hell. It is not just Bliss's face that comes to my mind. She is followed by BB's body in a toilet stall, Andrei, Miss Loretta, and poor Demarcus. Now, with the confirmation from Cohen, we know that Davis and Belle are dead, too. All dead in one night.

"Do you think Cohen is OK, bro?" Adam whispers. He, too, is resting against the wall with his eyes closed. It is a far cry from the normal cocky over-the-top person I have spent all summer with. Manda is breathing slowly, and I can't help but wonder if she is asleep. I hope so. We all need the rest.

"I don't know, Adam," I say back to him. "He has a gun. That has to count for something."

"I know, bro, but that first shot did nothing to him. It was like someone just flicked him with his finger." We both go quiet. I keep hoping that Cohen will be running up the steps and into the living room any moment. He would declare Able Dunn dead, and we can all get out of this nightmare.

"Bro," Adam says barely above a whisper. "I can't get past seeing BB's body." I can't register what is happening, but then it hits me that Adam is crying. My heart breaks at this. For all the cockiness and arrogance that he puts up for everyone else, he really is a softie. As I think back over the summer, he never really did anything to hurt me or try to embarrass me. I haven't stopped for a second to think about how this is affecting him.

"I spent two summers with him. He is my bro! We worked out together, partied together, and he even went home with me one weekend last year. My mom loved him. She kept telling me to be quiet and think more like BB. She wanted to adopt him by the end of the trip." Tears are still coming down his cheeks, but he starts to laugh.

"We were there over the Fourth of July. We spent the time drinking hard lemonade and swimming in my pool. We have a killer pool at our house. My dad is obsessed with swimming, and he designed this famous pool. It had rock designs, the lights underwater, and even a hot tub. Man, I had some good times there. BB loved the water, bro. He swam the whole morning." His eyes were open now, and I could see him looking off, remembering the moment.

"My mom went all out for BB. She was a beast that day. Food kept coming out of the kitchen. Burgers, brats, dogs, egg salad. Everything we could ask for. BB made a huge deal about my mom's chocolate chip banana pancakes. "Get this," Adam says. "Mrs. Jacobs, these are the best pancakes I have ever had." I must have looked shocked because he perked up. "No, I'm serious! That is the most I have ever heard him speak in two years. At least when he wasn't in coach mode." We both smile, thinking about quiet, mild-mannered BB riding some poor soul who was being lazy. Maybe he used up all his allotted words coaching, so he didn't have any left for social times.

"My mom made them all day. He would be swimming, and it seemed like every hour on the hour, my mom would bring out another stack of pancakes. BB's face would light up each and every time, bro. He would hop out of the pool and hug my mom, wet and all. My mom loved it. He would scarf down the cakes and jump right back in. It was a great day."

"My town has an old bridge that is no longer in commission, and each year, they would do a fireworks show on it. They would set them off over the river, and it's spectacular. The whole town comes out for it. Everyone starts gathering well before dark. BB came downtown with me, and he was a rock star, bro. Here was a true all-American football player in our small town. He was so kind, taking pictures with whoever wanted one. The kids there looked up to him so much. It was magical...and now he's gone." Adam really starts to cry then. I let him. I sit in silence with tears coming down my face, too. For BB, for Bliss, Demarcus, Miss Loretta, everyone.

"You sure are sexy when you cry," Manda says, not opening her eyes. We all break out laughing. I'm sure Adam thought she was asleep, like I did. She reaches and pecks Adam on the cheek. Her hand crosses over and takes mine in hers. What a group we make. The survivors of a vicious attack. Our leader is dead, our friends are dead, and we have yet to escape. The moment is nice, calming, and intimate.

Then, it all changes.

CHAPTER TWENTY-SIX

A loud crash explodes, and a body is tossed through the living room window.

It is Cohen.

At least I think it is Cohen. The head is nothing more than a flappy ball of hair and blood, but the body is his. Everything starts to move in slow motion. Manda starts to scream, her hands coming to her head and her teeth, pure white, showing all as she yells. I watch as Adam jumps up, bat in hand. He is saying something to me, but I can't understand what he is saying. I look across the room at Cohen's body lying next to Cook's. I can't seem to figure out what is going on. Manda is being pulled off the floor by Adam. She has dropped the axe, and he is picking it up and handing it to her. Again, I see him mouthing words to me.

"GET UP, BRO!" I hear him say, and the whole world comes back to me in a rush. Everything now speeds up. I jump to my feet, holding the machete that I carried from the Main House. Adam pulls me over to Manda, and we all turn to face the front door.

Able Dunn is standing in the doorway.

Lightning and thunder erupt behind me, making him look larger than he already is. His hulking frame is menacing, and his jacket is riddled with bullet holes. I am amazed. How did he survive getting shot that many times? He doesn't even look hurt. His chest is heaving, and he stares at us through the gas mask. I dare a glance at Adam, who gives me a short nod.

"For BB," I say.

"For Bliss, bro," he replies.

"For everyone," Manda says.

I feel courage rise in me, and I know that the whole night, maybe my whole life, has come down to this. All the years of the teasing, enduring the fat jokes, the shame, the rejection. All the embarrassment of never kissing a girl, never having a girlfriend, never even having a real date. This right here, right now, is my time. I found a home this summer, a true best friend, and a family. This psycho, this monster, this...killer has taken all of it from me. Now here I stand with the only two remaining family members left, and we have to do what no one else has been able to do this entire night.

"Let's kill this guy," I say.

I watch as Dunn takes a step into the room. Slow steps, deliberate. He seems to be calculating his odds. Three college-age students, all holding weapons, stand across from him. So far tonight, he has taken out a slob of a cook, an all-American athlete, and an old man with a gun. What could we possibly do?

Dunn continues to move toward us, and we start to slide toward the kitchen with our backs still against the wall. Dunn turns and stares as we move. If I could see his eyes, I am sure they are following us. The machete is heavy in my hand. I have never used a machete before, so I am going with the logic that you swing it fast and hard, and start chopping away at whatever you can. We bypass the kitchen because there is more space in Cohen's living room than in the white kitchen. With only the chair in the corner and a bookshelf along one wall, we can spread out a little more. For the time being, we stay put, shoulder-to-shoulder, touching each other. Safety in numbers.

"So, what is the plan here?" I ask.

"Kill him, bro."

"What is taking him so long? Why isn't he attacking us?" Manda says. She is right. Dunn has been staring us down for a full five minutes now and has yet to make a move. I can't tell if it is a predator stalking its prey or a cold, calculating monster waiting. Either way, it is nauseating waiting for this. We are three students working at a glorified summer camp. We are not hunters. We are not trained in this.

I went hunting one time in my life with my grandfather. I hated it from the very second it started. I don't like getting up early. I never have. So, when my grandpa woke me up at 4:30 a.m. and told me it was time to go, I didn't enjoy it. I was in fifth grade at the time, and I made some passing comment that all my friends were hunting, and I never got to go. My dad didn't like guns, so it was always my mom's side of the family who made sure I got the "manly stuff." My dad's side was into the arts. Singing, musical instruments, and theater were their areas of expertise. Farming, camping, fishing, and now hunting fell to my mother's side.

There I was up at 4:30 a.m., given this bar of protein to eat. The taste was similar to dry bark covered in more dry bark. It was freezing outside, that bone-chilling cold that only comes when it is pitch black outside and nothing else in the world is moving, so the cold just comes and rests on you. I was wearing a too-small camouflage outfit that my cousin had outgrown, but it was still too small for me, despite him being 5 years older. Oh, the joys of being big all your life.

We drove out to the middle of nowhere. We parked, and

my grandfather headed to the back of the truck to retrieve the guns. I stayed put, cursing myself for saying that I wanted to try hunting. He knocked on my window and waved at me to come along. I got out and followed him into the darkness. We walked for what seemed like two miles, which made me hate it even more since I hated walking. We finally came to this little shack. My grandfather climbed up into it, and I followed.

Inside was nothing but two little chairs and a bucket. I sat on one of the chairs and waited for my instructions. My grandfather explained to me that we still can't make a noise and looked out the opening to see a deer. When do we take a shot? The bucket was for going to the bathroom. It just got better.

It wasn't until the sun started to come up that we saw the first deer. I got excited because something was happening, and I got to finally shoot a gun. I was wrong. My grandpa explained to me that this was my first time, so I didn't actually get to shoot anything. I was to observe and learn. That was the final straw. We didn't make another hour, as I was complaining nonstop about the cold, the fact that I didn't get to shoot, and the boredom. Man, the boredom. The first deer we saw wasn't deemed big enough to mess with, so we let it go on its way. There hadn't been a sighting of another one since. My grandpa gave up, and we went to get pancakes. Something I was finally excited about.

I remember all this, and I am cursing myself again for not sticking it out, for not becoming a hunter, a real man. This is not a video game, and this isn't theater. I am here to fight for my life and the lives of my friends. There is no boredom here. Able Dunn is biding his time to see who he is going to go for first.

He chooses me.

CHAPTER TWENTY-SEVEN

Dunn starts toward me so fast that I am not ready. Instead of moving toward him with the machete raised and ready to attack, I move backward, scared out of my wits. When he gets to me, I watch as his big meat-hooked hand grabs me by the neck. His hand is pure rock, his fingers so long that they wrap around my large neck. The squeeze is so tight and vicious that my vision starts to fade almost instantly. He lifts me off the ground like nothing and tosses me out the front door.

I land hard and hit my head against the frame, but somehow I am still holding on to the machete. This all takes place in a span of 30 seconds or less, but to me, it's all taking an eternity. My stomach drops, as it often does when I have pain. I am so dizzy, I don't know what to do.

Dunn doesn't stop. He charges at me. I am not sure if it is pure reflex or everything is moving so fast that I don't have time to think, but right as he gets to me and reaches down, I pull the machete up in front of me and stab him in the shoulder. It's just driving a nail through frozen wood, but it does enough to stop him, and I think it surprises him. It sure surprised me. His momentum can't be slowed, and the machete is driving in deep.

This gives Adam his chance. He crosses over the room and starts pounding away on Dunn. He strikes in the back with the bat and then back down on the back of his head. Manda wakes up, too, and takes the axe to the back of Dunn's knee, dropping him down. I let go of the machete as he moves back. Before Adam can score another blow, Dunn stands up, turns, and catches the bat with his left hand, in mid-swing. Adam looks stunned.

Dunn rips the bat from Adam's grip and throws it on the ground. Then, with his right hand, he reaches up and grabs Adam by his throat. I know how it feels. He picks Adam up and throws him ALL THE WAY through the door across the room into the bookcase. Adam hits with a force that crushes the middle shelf, sending books falling all over Adam. I see a gash open up on his head. He lies motionless. I watch as Dunn slowly pulls the machete out of his shoulder, blood dripping off it as he makes his way over to Adam. He lifts the machete in the air.

Manda continues to fight. With a giant scream, she drives the axe into Dunn's back. She tries to pull it out, but it sticks. Dunn drops the machete and stands up straight. The axe is sitting on his back. He turns to face Manda. She starts to back up into the living room, and Dunn moves toward her. At this point, my brain starts swirling. I stand up and reach for the axe. I yank it out and then swing at his side. I hit it with all my force, and it knocks Dunn in the side. I follow that up with another swing into his knee, and he drops to the floor, resting on his knees. I swing for his head but miss, and the axe lands in his shoulder. I pick up the axe and wait, scanning the room. I see the bat on the ground by my feet. I pick it up and grip it hard.

I really hate football. Maybe I should clarify that I like

watching football at times. The game can be fun. But when it comes to organized teams, I hate it. Being big, everyone thinks you should play football. Not only play football, but I love it. From the moment I walked into junior high, all I heard from the coaches was, "I can't wait until I get you on the football field." At first, I thought I was special and that they really wanted me to play. But I found out quickly that I am not made for the sport.

It is so much running. I really hate running. When the season started, it was so hot. The pads were uncomfortable, and then I realized that all I was going to do was block people. Being an offensive lineman has to be the single most boring position ever created. You never get to touch the ball, you don't get to tackle people, and I always dreamed of being the kicker. Actually, I was the best kicker on the team, but I never got to do it in the game because "Fat boys don't kick, they block!" I hated that coach.

So, I never played. I quit after the first game of the season, in which I didn't even get to play. I realized that this sport is dumb. Plus, the coaches were sick of me asking why I couldn't kick, why I couldn't play defense, and, of course, the running. Throughout high school and even now in college, people will say something about how I needed to be on the field, how I am wasting my size by not playing football. I even stopped going to the games. I found my love in the arts. Being creative, thrilling a crowd, and no running. I hated football.

But I LOVE baseball. Love it. The best sport on the planet. Best sport ever created. The same grandfather who tried his best to get me to hunt also instilled the love of baseball into me. He gave me my first glove, took me to my first game, and taught me how to throw a fastball. I played all through high school. Yes, there is running in baseball, but not covered in dirty, nasty pads. So, now, as I stand here in Cohen's cabin gripping this baseball bat, I realize football could never prepare you for trying to kill a psycho. I raised the bat and swung away.

Right up against Able Dunn's head.

CHAPTER TWENTY-EIGHT

I haven't hit many home runs in my day. My first one came in first grade during my last year of Little League. I remember it as not only my first but also the only one-hit song that year in our town. I had saved my money all summer and bought a new bat called "The Thumper." It was the first game where I could use it.

It was the final game of the summer, and we were playing for first place. I batted eighth in the lineup, something my coach called "second clean up," but really it was because I was slow. I could hit, but could not run. As I stepped into the batter's box during my first at bat, I was all pride as I showed The Thumper to the catcher.

"That's a stupid bat," he said.

I dug in, and when the first pitch came at me, I swung away. I hit a long, high fly to the opposite field. I actually stood there watching it because I knew I hit it well.

"Run, JAMES!" I heard the dugout call, and I took off toward first base. I saw the ball sail over the right field fence as I turned, and the crowd went crazy. Friday night baseball in a small town where nothing goes on during the summer always draws a crowd. This was the first home run of the entire summer. As I approached second base, I jumped in the air and stomped the bag with both feet. My coach was all smiles and going crazy as I turned toward home. I touched the plate and looked right in the catcher's face.

"What a stupid bat, huh?" I said, and then went to celebrate with my teammates. I still have that ball at home. A lady in the stands got the ball and inscribed the date, time, and place on it for me. I love that thing. You see, the one thing I remember about hitting that ball is the sound and the feel of the ball when it hit the bat. The only way to describe it is the perfect, solid hit. I never forgot that feeling.

When I connected against Dunn's head, I felt the same way.

His head plowed sideways ahead of the rest of the body, which soon joined him on the floor. I saw blood ooze out from under the gas mask. I stood over him holding the bat. I felt like a giant. Manda had stopped backing up and was looking at me in awe. This bat was no Thumper, but it did the trick. I looked at the barrel covered in blood and let it drop to the floor. I went and grabbed Manda, and we made our way over to check on Adam.

He is starting to move a little.

Manda and I started cleaning all the books and wood off him. I was thankful the gash on his head wasn't as bad as it looked. He was covered in dust and looked dazed. I don't think these books have been read in ages. What was Cohen doing? Just looking at them? Manda gets a wet cloth from the kitchen and we lean Adam against the broken shelf. Manda starts cleaning up the gash on his hand.

"What happened, bro?" I laugh. Even in pain and with a possible concussion, Adam is still the same. "I feel like a truck hit me." He starts to cough, and dust shakes off his head. Manda removes the cloth and kisses him on the cheek.

"Able Dunn tossed you across the room, dear."

"Bro?" Adam says, looking at me. "Across the room?"

"Like you were nothing, man. I'm sorry." He looks like he doesn't believe a word we are saying, and I can't blame him. Adam is a big dude, a true athlete. He looks past me and notices Dunn lying still on the floor.

"What happened there?" he says to no one.

"James here went all Babe Ruth on Able."

"BRO! Really?" Adam gets a big grin on his face. "Have you been holding out on me all summer?" I laugh and give him a nod. We all start to laugh.

"You should have seen him, Adam. He has a great swing." Adam punches me in the shoulder.

"No way, bro. You like baseball?"

"Love it. Best sport on the planet."

"Why didn't you ever say anything? Or play in any of the pick-up games?" Adam looks genuinely hurt. I can't help but start laughing at this whole conversation.

"You never asked me, bro," I say back, and this sets us all off laughing again. We spend a few minutes laughing and feeling calm.

"I guess it's something else I have to apologize for, along with giving you that nickname all summer."

"It's OK, man. We are good." Adam leans his head back and smiles. I have seen that smile all summer, and this is the most genuine I have seen it. No pretense, no pressure, no facade. I guess having your body tossed across the room and crashing into a bookcase will do it. Either that or he is high from all the book dust he inhaled. Manda and I are covered in it as well. Along with blood, mud, and whatever comes out of bodies. I am not looking forward to doing laundry. Maybe I will take some of the money from this summer and get some new clothes. Clothes for big people are very expensive.

"You wanna try and stand?" I ask Adam. "Take it easy, though. You might have a concussion."

"Bro, I have had so many concussions they don't even faze me anymore."

"That doesn't sound medically accurate."

"I'm good. Help me up." Easier said than done. We have to try two or three times to get him up. His legs are weak, and no matter what he says, he doesn't seem coherent. But we get him standing, and he looks relieved to be off the floor.

"I love you guys," he says, smiling at us.

But the smile doesn't last long.

CHAPTER TWENTY-NINE

"NO!" Adam's eyes grow wide, and he pushes us out of the way, knocking us to the ground. As we hit the floor, I look to see Dunn charging toward Adam. The machete I dropped is in his hand. He stabs Adam deep in the shoulder, driving him all the way back into the wall. Dunn pulled the machete back out, and Adam slumped to the ground. He doesn't move. Dunn turns around and looks right at me. I guess he knows who hit him in the head with a baseball bat.

He charges, and this time I don't freeze. I roll over and grab the baseball again. I jump up, grip the bat, and stand ready. Dunn stops. I don't think he was ready for me to do a move like a ninja. I'm pretty agile for a person my size when I am motivated. The distraction is wonderful as Manda takes this chance to attack with her axe once again. She is more prepared this time. She hits Dunn in between the shoulder blades and pulls it out before it gets stuck this time. She lands another blow a little lower. Unlike before, Dunn shows the pain this time. He is weakening.

I go in and nail him in the side with the bat. He falters

but doesn't quite fall all the way. Manda continues to attack his back and legs. This must have annoyed him because he turns to face her. She doesn't back down, either, and she drives the axe down into Dunn's chest hard. I see blood splatter out and cover her. Now that I am behind him, I swing the bat down vertically onto the back of the gas mask. This finally drops Dunn.

We don't stop.

We both keep attacking. At first, Dunn is fighting, moving, trying to block our blows. The blows from the axe and the bat are working as we ravage him. Blood oozes out of the front of Dunn's body, and his mask is caved in. Even after he stops moving, we keep up the attack. We will leave no doubt this time. I want to finish Able Dunn for good.

I don't even know how long we keep it up, but finally, Manda and I collapse with exhaustion. Even with the attacks, Dunn is still moving. Like a weakened giant, he stands up one last time. How is he still alive? I don't have time to think about it because I hear a yell and look to see Adam charge across the room. He spears Dunn and takes him out through the entire living room wall! Manda and I sit astonished at what we witnessed. All we can see through the hole in the wall is dust and Adam's body standing over Able Dunn. I take back what I said about football preparing you for a night like this. The excitement doesn't last long as we see Adam collapse. We both rush through the hole onto the porch. I see Dunn's body lying in a heap with Adam's body on top.

"How is Adam?" I ask in between heavy breaths. Manda reaches down to him. She checks him for a pulse.

"He is alive," she says. A deep relief comes over me. I don't think I could have handled another death. Manda, being braver than I could imagine, reaches down and checks the pulse on the other body. Her hand comes up to her face.

"There's no pulse." She says, turning to look at me. Her eyes are wide. "He is dead!"

I am on the dirty, dusty porch, covered in a pool of blood, and I don't care. We are alive. Dunn is dead. The carnage has ended. I work hard to catch my breath. I am in a dream-like state when Manda comes over to me.

"We should get out of here," I say.

"Couldn't have said it better myself." She gives me that million-dollar smile. She helps me up, and we go over to retrieve Adam. The pain awakens him as I put his bad shoulder over mine.

"Ouch, bro!" he yells. "That hurts."

"Sorry, man. You were stabbed with a machete."

"Feels like it." He winces at any movement.

Manda takes his other arm over her shoulder and heads down the steps. The rain has stopped again. We take our time going down the steps that lead off the porch. It's a little way before we can get on the wooden path that runs through the camp. The mud is slick, and Adam is barely walking. We have to stop at the gazebo to rest a bit. The exhaustion is real.

"Is he dead?" Adam asks, lying on a bench, eyes closed.

"Yes," is all Manda says. I hear Adam let out a sigh. I feel the same way. We all sit there. Not wanting to move another inch, but knowing we need to get out of there.

We start moving again. It is even harder moving up the steps to the Main House. They are slick, and I have this awful vision of all of us falling down the steps and breaking our necks. That would be just the worst. But we don't. When we reach the top of the steps, we have to stop and rest again. We take a long look at the back door of the Main House. Its dark doorway looks as menacing as ever. Not warm and welcoming like it once was, like it was earlier this very night.

"I can't go back in there," Manda says. No one says anything, but we all agree and bypass around to the front. We notice the police car right away. We pick up our steps and head in that direction. Help is finally here. But again, it wasn't. We find Officer Spencer's body on the side of the car by the open driver's door. The only way we knew it was him was from his name tag.

"Let's take my truck," I say. No one argues. We move to the road where we park our vehicles during the week. My truck is exactly how I left it. The sight of her makes me want to cry. It is a symbol of a simpler time. A time before Able Dunn. I get settled behind the steering wheel with Adam in the middle of us. Manda piles in.

She starts up with ease. I hit the wipers to wash away the water and turn the headlights on. I give her a second to warm up, and I start to back up. I turn, and we start to head out of Camp NoTech.

"Feel free to speed things up, bro. I might be dying."

"I don't think you are dying," I hear Manda answer.

"Are you suggesting uber speed?" I ask him. We all laugh.

"Just lean up against me and try to get some rest. The last thing we need is to die by trying to drive out of here fast." I laugh and push the gas a little harder. I see the lights of the Camp NoTech sign up ahead. I can't help but wonder if it is the last time I will ever see it. If anyone will ever see it. My heart breaks for the loss of Miss Loretta. She poured her heart and soul into this place. She didn't deserve the end she got or the end to her camp. We ease our way down the road.

Someone is standing in our way.

CHAPTER THIRTY

"**Y**ou have got to be kidding me, bro!"

Able Dunn stands in our way. He is bloody and barely standing, but there he is. Holding the axe left in Cohen's cabin, he looks determined. Hiding behind a mask makes it hard to read his face, but I am pretty sure he is pissed at us. I can't imagine that getting beaten down with a baseball bat and an axe would make one happy.

"Why won't he die?" Manda screams. I have come to a complete stop about 30 yards away from him. The truck is idling, headlights shining bright on him. I don't think he is going to move.

"Hit him, bro. Take the truck and crush him!" This makes me sick to my stomach. I have spent the last six years of my life taking care of this truck. I don't want to ruin it, with all the work and money gone into it, by trying to stop this guy. Again. My hesitation is showing, and I feel Manda reaching over and tapping me on the shoulder.

"James? Any time now."

I start running through scenarios of my options. One, hit Able Dunn and hope this finally does the trick. Two, we wait him out. Maybe his injuries will get the best of him, perhaps he will even get bored and want to leave. Three, head back into the camp and hope he follows us and we lose him again. Last, we can get out and try to take him down one more time. None of these sound appealing.

I try to work up the courage to lower the stick and charge forward. I picture everyone from tonight. Cook, BB, Lin, Demarcus, Andrei, Miss Loretta, Officer Spencer, Cohen, and Bliss. The last face, the face of my true best friend, pushes me over the head. I lower the stick and start to rev the engine.

"That's it, bro," Adam yells. "Go for it, man. Do it, DO IT!"

I hit the gas and peel out. Dunn starts to charge toward us. I feel the tire take traction, and we jerk forward. I speed up as fast as the old girl goes. I've only done this one other time, when I stupidly tried to race my cousin one summer. I nearly died. Promised myself I would never try it again. A promise now to be broken. We are nearly at 50 miles per hour when I see Dunn raise the axe. He is swinging and aiming to hit the engine.

But he is too slow.

I hit him dead on, and he flips over the hood and lands in the back of the truck. I skidded to a stop. I look at the others.

"What do I do?" I ask.

"No way he survived that, bro. Let's get out of here."

"Like now," Manda adds. I drop the lever and take off again.

I don't dare to slow down until we start to rise out of the valley. The road is harder going out of camp than it is coming down into the valley. Steeper and more treacherous. As much as my adrenaline is racing and we want to escape, I have to force myself to go slowly.

None of us is speaking. Adam is passed out on Manda,

who is staring out the window. There has been no movement out of Dunn since he landed. My eyes constantly shift from the road to the mirror, searching for any hint that he might still be alive. I am taking nothing for granted. We take the first big turn and continue upward.

The drive out of camp takes a while. You never get cell reception until the very top. Saturdays were our only day off at Camp NoTech, and it was always thrilling to see what messages and texts will appear once we get back to cell phone range. Since my mom doesn't text, I am the one who usually has the most voicemails. My mom has a thing about leaving me a message every night of the week. She tells me about her day, about how proud of me she is, how our dog is doing, and the ladies at church. She feels like it connects her to me since I can't actually speak to her during the week. Everyone teases me about the voicemails, but in secret, I love them. I did make the mistake of playing one aloud for everyone, in which my mom went into detail about the problems she was having with her bowels. Demarcus said he had something he could cook up for her to cure the problem.

Miss Loretta made us all spend a Saturday together twice each summer. It's all the campers, herself, and Cohen. Rumor has it that Cook was made to go one time but hated it so much she threatened to quit. We all piled into the camp bus for team bonding, which that day happened to be a trip to a water park. As we made our way out of the camp, Andrei invented "Cell Phone Blitz."

The object of the game is simple. Everyone turns their phone on, and we all wait to see whose will alert first. The first one to get a voicemail or text to pop up is the winner and doesn't have to pay for their meals that day. It was a blast and pretty intense. No one could figure out why, but Lin's cell phone always won. So, now the tradition was set. Anytime any of us left for the day, we would all play. Every once in a while, you would get an alert really early up the road, but most of the time, you have to be almost out of the valley to get anything.

"Do you guys want to play cell phone blitz?" I ask. This must have struck a chord because Manda starts laughing hard. I am soon joining her. Adam opens his eyes to us, laughing our heads off. Manda pulls out her phone and starts to power it up. I do the same.

"My phone is in my pocket, bro." I reach down and get his phone out. It is busted.

"No, bro! My phone!" which makes us laugh all the harder. Adam is the most useless person when it comes to technology. Something that we all think is why he loves Camp NoTech so much. He has the latest and most expensive smartphone, but he has no clue how to use it. But at this moment, he looks like his puppy died. Poor guy.

"I don't have anything yet," Manda says. I check the mirror one more time and then look at my phone.

"Same here."

"I don't have anything either, bro," which sets off another laughing fit. Manda is crying tears when she lets out a yelp.

"My texts just came through."

"Call 911," I say. She enters the password and opens to the home screen. She punches in the number, and we all wait. It seems like forever.

"Yes. Yes, um, this is Manda, and I am one of the counselors at Camp NoTech. We need your help. There has been a bunch of people killed." She pauses. "Yes, you heard me. And a fire. And Officer Spencer is dead." Another pause. "Where am I? I am with two other counselors, one is very hurt, and we are almost out of the valley." She is silent for a minute. "Ok, I will." She puts her hand over her mouth and says,

"They want me to stay on the phone with them. Head into town, and they will meet us on the way with an ambulance."

"Awesome." I nod and check the mirror one more time.

Able Dunn is moving.

CHAPTER THIRTY-ONE

I can see the blacktop, and I gun the engine and take the last corner fast, almost tipping the truck on two wheels. Once I am settled on the road, I bring her up as fast as she can go.

"What are you doing, James?" I hear Manda scream. The windows are down, and now that we are going fast, it is loud.

"He is not dead."

"What do you mean not dead, bro?"

Before I can answer, Dunn busts his fist through the back windshield. He grabs Adam and starts to pull him out of the bed of the truck. I am going well over 80, but I let go of the wheel with my right hand and start to fight to bring him back in.

"Help me, bro!" Adam screams, and Dunn is scraping his back against the broken glass of the windshield. Blood is starting to come through his shirt where the glass is cutting. Adam, to his credit, is fighting as hard as I am. Manda has twisted her body around and is kicking at Dunn. She is having the best luck out of all of us in this truck.

I am having trouble keeping the truck straight while using my free hand to fight. Where is a machete when you need one? My feet are getting tangled, and the gas pedal is getting pressed harder, making us speed up more. Dunn has Adam about halfway out the back. I lose control of the wheel for a second, and we are flying off into a long ditch that runs along the side of the road. I have no choice but to grab the wheel and fight to get us back on the road. The ditch is a tough terrain, and it jerks the wheels of the truck all over, which actually helps us as it causes Dunn to lose control. Adam falls back into the cab of the truck and tries to curl up into a ball.

Manda is still kicking at Dunn. I manage to get the truck back on the road. As I do, we are driving head-on toward another truck. The other driver swerves to try and avoid us, but I hit the back end. My truck bangs it hard, causing us to flip. Then, I am sent upside down with everyone else. No one is wearing their seatbelt. The truck lands on its side. I am on the bottom, and we are scraping across the pavement. We come to rest after about 10 yards, and everything goes black.

I am underwater.

I feel nothing; I am weightless.

I see a light far above me.

I know I need to swim for it, but I am way too tired.

I don't want to go back.

"Son? Son, can you hear me?" I come back to the world, looking at a police officer looking at me. I feel myself being wheeled on a bumpy cart. My head is killing me, and the light is so bright. I move to cover my eyes with my hand and realize that there is liquid all over it. It is now all over my face.

Blood.

Everything comes back to me at sonic speed. Bliss, BB, Miss Loretta, Andrei, Cohen. Manda, Adam...

"Manda! Adam!" I scream, trying to sit up, and my body rejects that idea. The pain is intense. "Sir, SIR!" I yell at the officer. "Where are my friends?" I am starting to become frantic. After all we've been through, if I were to lose them now...

"I'm right here, James." Manda comes into my view, and she grabs my hand. She looks like an angel. Nothing seems to be wrong with her at all. Not a scratch.

"Adam?" I say.

"He's fine. Well, still really banged up and hurt, but he is OK. It was a miracle, James. I don't know how we survived that. " I collapse back on the cart.

"You look perfect," I say. She laughs at me. She lifts her other arm, and I see that she has an inflatable cast on it. I start to laugh, but my body rejects that, too.

"They say you are fine. You are going to be sore for a while and will be the poster child for the term 'bumps and bruises,' but overall, you are totally OK." With that news, I lay back and close my eyes. I can feel them wheeling to a stop to start the process of lifting me into the back of the ambulance. I hear Manda ask if she can ride with me, and she is granted permission.

"Thank you, Manda." She gives my hand a tight squeeze. They settled me in, and we take off. The pain is starting to hit me now, and I am so exhausted. Manda lets me know a call has already been made to my mom. She is en route, and another laugh escapes me. My mom is a maniac behind the wheel and will make the five-hour drive in less than three. Soon, she will take over the hospital and start bossing everyone around. But it makes me feel great inside.

Manda reassures me that Adam is going to be fine, and we are all headed to the hospital in Rock Creek. This day finally looks to be done. Then, my stomach drops into my feet.

"Manda," I say, sitting up this time, despite the pain. "Is he dead? Is Able Dunn dead?" Manda looks at me with a grave look on her face, her eyes stone serious.

"James," Manda says. "They can't find Able Dunn anywhere."

EPILOGUE

I park my car in my assigned spot, but I don't turn off the motor. It is freezing on the campus of Mountain College, and I am not ready to face the blizzard that is starting outside. It is going to be a big one; the forecasters are predicting a record number for snowfall. I love the snow, and the thought of being snowed in over Easter break is awesome. There is nothing I love more than being bundled up in a warm house with plenty of food, movies to watch, games to play, and being with your friends while the world is a blanket outside.

Usually, I would be on my way home for Easter right now, but after transferring to MC, my mom doesn't want me driving the eight hours, not after "all I have been through." I guess being chased around a camp while seeing all your fellow counselors get murdered disqualifies me from long car rides. But I am more than happy to stay here with the rest of the folks at The Castle.

No, it is not a real castle. It is a very old house out in the countryside of Mountain View, where MC is located. It is a crazy big house built to hold the entire Knox family; the founders of not only MC or Mountain View, but all of Miller County. Over the years, they kept adding onto it so the whole Knox clan could live under one giant roof. The college purchased it a few years ago and turned it into a sorority and fraternity house. Yes, I, James, left my small private school to be brave on the big campus of MC, AND become a member of the proud fraternity known as Omega Ki Omega.

After everything happened at Camp NoTech, I was in the Rocky Creek hospital for three weeks before I was allowed to return home. Adam was there even longer than that. By the time I was home and well, the semester had started. Manda, Adam, and I became the best of friends. We all three took the semester off. When it was time to start up again, we both transferred to MC to be closer and help Adam, who was still recovering and doing hours of therapy. Adam did what Adam does, and without any hazing, I became a full brother. Manda joined the sorority that occupies the other half of the house, and here we are.

It didn't end there. Two of our campers from NoTech came with us. Tommy Hitts practically moved into the hospital to take care of us. Through the process, he decided he wanted to be a nurse. MC has an excellent program, so he joined us. Joined the frat and lives in The Castle too. Raven Giles is here, too. After everything broke, she called or Face-timed me every day. In the spirit of Camp NoTech, she also wrote me letters. Real letters, like on paper, with stamps and everything. She too came to MC to join us. While not part of the sorority, she spends all her time with us.

I have feelings. Bad.

The massacre at Camp NoTech became national news. It is not every day that a killing spree like that happens. Throw in an all-American football player as one of the victims, and the story was too good not to cover. Thankfully, our names, the sole survivors, were never released to the public. This spared us from an onslaught of another kind. Miss Loretta's family sold off the land and all the properties to a weight loss camp. Strong security was put in place, cell towers built, and high-speed internet dragged down into the valley. They were not going to be cut off from the outside world. Miss Loretta went the extra mile, covering all our medical bills and giving us each a final "bonus" that will pay for all our school and then some.

Able Dunn was never found. No trace was left of him besides a trail of blood that led off into a cornfield. No places were found to show where he had been living or hiding during the years before the attack. If he is alive, no one knows. But the fat camp will be ready if he returns. They employ a 10-man team that patrols the camp at all times. If anything, those people can lose weight running for their lives.

Speaking of weight, I am down 50 pounds. It all started with the terrible hospital food, continued when I got home, and really kicked into high gear when I moved into The Castle. Adam loves nothing more than being my personal trainer, and he is determined to get me on the baseball team next year. At first, I hated getting up early (don't like), running (double don't like), and eating less was not fun. But it has paid off. Manda says that the girls will be all over me soon, even though there is really only one I have my eye on. Feelings. Bad.

So, I am not going home for Easter, my favorite holiday, but I will be spending cozy and warm days with my two best friends and two others who have become family to us. The snow is just a bonus. I'm sure with Adam, there will be chaos, naked snow angels, massive snowball fights inside and outside, and more than one game of find the snake in Adam's pants. Here is a hint: sometimes there is actually a real, live snake in Adam's pants. I have found my true friends, some true brothers, a true sister, perhaps even a girl,

All it took was a night of hell to find heaven.

The End